KT-417-468

DEVIL'S

DEVIL'S BOUNTY

KEN HODGSON

PINNACLE BOOKS
Kensington Publishing Corp.
http://www.kensingtonbooks.com

This book is a work of fiction. Names, characters, places, and incidents are either the product of the author's imagination, or are used fictitiously. Any resemblance to actual persons, living or dead, or events is entirely coincidental.

All Kensington Titles, Imprints, and Distributed Lines are available at special quantity discounts for bulk purchases for sales promotions, premiums, fund-raising, and educational or institutional use. Special book excerpts or customized printings can also be created to fit specific needs. For details, write or phone the office of the Kensington special sales manager: Kensington Publishing Corp., 850 Third Avenue, New York, NY 10022, attn: Special Sales Department, Phone: 1-800-221-2647.

Pinnacle and the P logo Reg. U.S. Pat. & TM Off.

First Pinnacle Books Printing: May 2006

10 9 8 7 6 5 4 3 2 1

Printed in the United States of America

This book is for Elmer Kelton.

If you prick us, do we not bleed? If you tickle us, do we not laugh? If you poison us, do we not die? And if you wrong us, shall we not revenge?

Shakespeare, *The Merchant of Venice*
Act III, Sc. i

Chapter 1

Three days out of San Angelo, Sam Flatt's head began to draw flies. The bounty hunter swatted at the smelly saddlebag with his hat, wiped sweat from his forehead onto his sleeve, then returned the Bollinger to his head and pulled the wide brim low over his eyes. Ahead, the rolling cactus-studded badlands of West Texas undulated in the summer heat like a waterless ocean for as far as the eye could see.

"I should have been a corset salesman," Dallas Handley muttered to himself. "Putting up with finicky women would be a sight more pleasant task than chasing after outlaws, especially in unfavorable weather."

Dallas fished a small leather-covered brass telescope from the other saddlebag, clicked it into focus, and carefully scanned the barren landscape. Aside from a distant dust devil winding its way across a low valley, the bounty hunter saw nothing else moving in the stifling morning heat.

He folded the telescope closed and tucked it away. With a flick of the reins he put the gelding into a gentle trot, heading west for the town of Fort Stockton. No matter how badly he wanted to catch up with Jasper

Flatt, the brother of the man whose head he had in the saddlebag, hurrying was never a good idea in desert country. Water holes, even those that were well known, could become dry, or so laden with alkali that the water became unpalatable for man or beast.

Caution, along with a hard-won knowledge of how desperados behave, had not only kept Dallas alive for the past eleven years, it had also garnered him a reputation as a bounty hunter who always got his man, dead or alive. Dead was generally a lot less trouble.

At least when he got to Fort Stockton he could hand Sam Flatt's head over to Sheriff Perkins for identification and claim the two-thousand-dollar reward. The bounty hunter always hated it when circumstances forced him to improvise in this manner, especially in hot weather.

The bounty hunter had caught up with the Flatt brothers a few miles south of San Angelo alongside the Concho River. A well-placed slug from his Sharps rifle had ended the one outlaw's career. Jasper, however, was quicker and luckier than expected. The bank robber and murderer who was wanted in three states had not hesitated for even a heartbeat to drop, Indian-style, to the far side of his horse, grabbing the reins of his brother's mount as he did so, and gallop off down a sheltering draw, abandoning his flesh and blood to whatever fate decreed. This was one of the most cold-blooded acts Dallas had ever witnessed, confirming his belief that all wanted men were not to be trusted.

Having to tote around an entire dead outlaw while tracking another who happened to be worth another two thousand dollars was simply not a tolerable situation. It was messy work, since Dallas had been forced to use a small pocketknife for the task, but less than a half hour later he had washed up in the river and was in pursuit carrying along enough of Sam Flatt to claim the bounty. A few black turkey buzzards were already circling to clean up the remains when Dallas had ridden away.

Most sheriffs were of the understanding sort and seldom complained about having only a head to identify. Having fewer ornery crooks about gave them less to worry about, along with more time off to go fishing and enjoy life. Local undertakers also generally took the bounty hunter's side of any disagreements as they considered the less work they had to expend as a good bonus.

Bringing in only a head on occasion also had the salubrious effect of bandying about his reputation as a man not to be trifled with. These stories always became wonderfully blown out of proportion as they made their way from saloon to saloon, building fear in every wanted man who heard about the bloody bounty hunter, Dallas Handley, out of San Angelo, Texas. Putting fear in the dark hearts of outlaws had a tendency to make them nervous. And nervous men made mistakes.

Dallas would turn thirty-one his next birthday, yet since the summer of his sixteenth year, he had made his living in the rough-and-tumble state of Texas by subduing the outlaw element that grew, as his father was fond of saying, "like the loaves and fishes."

For the first three years he had been employed as a deputy under the stern eye of Sheriff Jack Stinson. The young lawman soon realized that pursuing and bringing to justice even the most worthless of outlaws paid better than the fifty dollars a month he received from Tom Green County. The decision to become a full-time bounty hunter was strictly a financial one. For the past eleven years it had been a quite lucrative one, buoyed by the fact he had yet to be seriously injured by any of the bloodthirsty outlaws that the West was noted for.

Now, with an assured two thousand dollars worth of outlaw tucked safely away in a saddlebag and another two-thousand-dollar bounty riding a horse only a few miles ahead, the seasoned bounty hunter continued his relaxed, deliberate pace as he rode west toward the railroad town of Fort Stockton.

Despite the late afternoon heat, Dallas felt the semblance of a chill on the nape of his neck when he rode the gelding onto the dusty main street of Fort Stockton. The sensation was akin to having the icy breath of the Grim Reaper blow down his shirt collar, and the experience was not a new one. For some unexplained reason, the bounty hunter received this as a warning, and one never to be ignored. It had saved his life many times.

Dallas reined the horse in the shadow of a two-story frame building, then drew to a halt. Normally, at this time of day, only a smattering of people would be seen out and about. This was not the case. Dozens of men were running about on the board sidewalks. What caught Dallas's full attention was that most of them were scurrying in and out of his destination: the sheriff's office.

It galled Dallas to think that he most likely had lost the second half of his bounty. Herbert Perkins, the sheriff of Pecos County, surely had been lucky enough to either capture or kill Jasper Flatt. Yet that situation did not explain the hairs on his neck standing on end like they were.

He dismounted, tied the reins to a hitching rail, and began making his way toward the milling crowd, keeping close to the buildings and in the shadows, his pale green eyes flashing about, alert as a cat on the hunt. As he approached the sheriff's office, Dallas instinctively held an open palm over the pearl handle of his .45 Colt Peacemaker. Something was *definitely* wrong.

A man wearing a white shirt with a black string tie yelled at a kid, "I don't care if the doc is passed out drunk. Throw a bucket of water on him and drag him down here. The deputy ain't dead yet."

When the wide-eyed boy ran past him, Dallas held out an arm. "What happened here, son?"

"The . . . the sheriff's been killed an' the bank president too. My pa owns the saloon. He thinks the deputy might make it if I hurry."

"Get on with it," Dallas said, already marching for the open door of the sheriff's office.

"Hold up there, stranger," a burly man wearing overalls said, stepping in front of him. "This is a matter for the law." He paled when Dallas faced him. "Oh, crap, you're that bounty hunter, Dallas Handley. I'll be begging your pardon, I didn't recognize you. As you can see, we're having a mighty troublesome day."

"No offense taken." Dallas nodded toward the open door. "I've been chasing an outlaw since San Angelo by the name of Jasper Flatt who is wanted for murder."

"I'd reckon he's done been here already," the white-shirted man said, stepping onto the boardwalk. He extended his hand. "Randall Evans. I own the Sour Mash Saloon just over there." He motioned to a false-front two-story building up the street where piano music was drifting from the batwing doors. "I grabbed my shotgun and come running when I heard all the commotion, but it was too late."

The man in overalls said, "No one thought anything odd when a thin feller leading a horse tied up to a rail and went inside the bank. That feller kilt Omar

Goldman right after he handed over all the money. Then when Sheriff Perkins an' Deputy Johnson came running out, this man simply cut them down before God got the news. Poor ol' Herb never knew what hit him."

"Jasper Flatt's known for such behavior," Dallas said. "That's why there's a two-thousand-dollar reward on his head."

"Have you had much experience with gunshot wounds?" Randall asked, stepping away from the open door. "Our local doc ain't worth much except in the mornings, and from the looks of things, the deputy's in no shape to wait until he's sober."

"I'll see if I can help," Dallas said on his way inside the sheriff's office. "The first thing to do is stop them from leaking blood."

Dallas Handley stifled a sigh when he bent to study the deputy, who lay on the floor in front of an oak desk. He figured the young man to be twenty years old at the most; his face was a contorted mask of pain. The bounty hunter thought briefly about pulling away from the wound the fallen lawman's hands, which were held tight to his bleeding belly, then decided it would be a futile gesture. He had seen too many men gut-shot to hold any hope for recovery.

"You hang in there, son," Dallas lied. "There ain't nothing vital been hit."

"I hurt bad." The deputy's voice came as a wet gurgle. "And I never even got a shot off."

"Just rest easy." Dallas noticed a thick puddle of blood spreading onto the plank floor from the lad's back. He knew the heavy-caliber slug had likely blown a hole the size of an egg where it had come out. "The man who shot you is Jasper Flatt and he's an outlaw of the worst sort. There's no way you could have known he would . . ."

The bounty hunter reverently reached out and brushed the deputy's eyelids closed. "And son," he said softly, "I *will* see him hang."

From the boardwalk Randall Evans hollered, "Here comes the doc."

Dallas stood and walked outside. The fiery orb of a dying sun was sinking into the western horizon leaving behind velvet fingers of shadows to grasp the remains of the day.

"Tell the sodden sawbones he can go back to his bottle." The bounty hunter blinked into the coming twilight. "And have the undertaker keep an extra coffin at the ready, because I intend to fill it with Jasper Flatt right soon."

Chapter 2

The smoldering fires of hate seared harshly in Dallas Handley's breast as he rode west beneath a twinkling canopy of stars. A wan half-moon gave ample light to guide his way along the dusty wagon road. *Sheriff Perkins was a decent man, and a fair one. He did not deserve to be shot down in cold blood. Hell, he never even got his gun out of his holster. Then again, neither did that poor kid of a deputy. They were all murdered, plain and simple. None of those three dead men back there stood a chance. They simply didn't know the type of man they were up against.*

A thin smile crossed the bounty hunter's face, turning up his trimmed black mustache at the ends. *But I do.*

It galled the bounty hunter that he had not been able to shoot both of the murdering brothers when he first caught up with them. *I should have ridden faster,* Dallas thought, then shook his head as if to toss away that idea. Hard experience had taught him to never push a horse too hard. An exhausted mount might step in a gopher hole or simply pull up lame from throwing a shoe. A slow deliberate pace was what it took for a successful manhunt. He *would* catch up with Jasper Flatt. And soon.

From the stable in back of the sheriff's office, Dallas had exchanged his gelding for a spirited pinto. Knowing the rugged mountainous area of West Texas where the pursuit could take him, he led a packhorse burdened with bags of water, ample supplies of beef jerky, salt, dried hot chili peppers, pinto beans, bacon that had been wrapped with vinegar-soaked cloth to keep it from spoiling, extra clothes, and, of course, an ample supply of ammunition for his Sharps rifle, Colt pistol, and the tiny Gem .22 revolver that he carried in a holster sewn inside his left boot.

Two of the usual items he carried, being one pair each of steel handcuffs and leg irons, he had marked with his initials and left at the sheriff's office. They were heavy and would not be used on this manhunt. Not after the carnage Jasper Flatt had wrought in Fort Stockton. The man was akin to a rabid animal and Dallas intended to rid Texas of this scourge in short order.

Dallas snorted when he gazed ahead up the moonlit wagon road and marveled at the plain trail Jasper Flatt was leaving. The horse the outlaw now rode—he had stolen a fresh mount from in front of the bank he'd robbed—had a shoe with one end pointed outward. Following his quarry was as simple as keeping an eye on the silvery railroad tracks of the newly laid Texas and New Orleans Railroad that paralleled the wagon road.

This situation gave him pause to consider. Either the outlaw did not realize he was being followed, a doubtful conclusion, or he was deliberately leaving a brazen trail hoping to lull his pursers into a false sense of security, then pull an ambush. There was even a fair possibility Jasper might circle around and come at him from his backside. Dallas remembered having briefly seen the stock of a rifle in a saddle holster.

"Situations like this are why I get paid the big money," he muttered to himself, a habit he had taken up years ago to relieve the stone silence of the prairies. "There are cactus plants out here smarter than Flatt. I simply need to pay attention."

Dallas noted the position of the moon and decided it was approaching the shank of bitter midnight. He took a long nine cigar from his vest pocket, and stuck it into his mouth. Chewing on a dead cigar always gave him a lift when he began to feel tired and sleepy. Just when he was preparing to bite off the end, a distant flicker of yellow light caused him to delay enjoying a chew.

He reined to a stop and employed his telescope to survey the distant light that now twinkled against the night like a low star. Through the lens Dallas studied the shack where a coal-oil lamp in the window was winking against the darkness. From the imposing wooden water tank that stood high above the tracks, Dallas knew this was a water stop for the railroad. Steam engines used copious amounts of both coal or wood and water on their trek across the West, necessitating numerous supply stations such as this one. This would also be a good time and place for an ambush. For all he knew, Jasper Flatt could have already killed the station attendants, then lit the lantern to attract him.

Dallas tucked the telescope away and dismounted. He tied the reins of the lead horse to a greasewood bush, then slid the Sharps rifle from its scabbard and assured himself a cartridge was chambered. From the saddlebag of his packhorse he grabbed a handful of long brass .40-caliber cartridges, tucking them away in the front pocket of his Levi's. Jasper wasn't the only one who could circle around and perform an ambush.

From the inky rounded hills to the south, a pack of coyotes sang their mournful song to the moon. Crick-

ets chirped their discordant tune, while an occasional
breeze rustled the scrawny brush that somehow managed to survive in the barren countryside. Aside from
the normal sounds of night in the desert, Dallas could
note nothing amiss.

The bounty hunter clenched his teeth on the cigar to
squeeze out the tobacco juice. He swallowed, then
moving as silently as the pale moon overhead, he melted
into the shadows of the raised railroad bed.

Dallas backtracked to where the light from the cabin
could not be seen before crossing to the other side of
the tracks. Keeping low, he took a circular path that
brought him a good half mile to the north. It was slow
going. Cactus were plentiful, as were loose rocks and
holes made by various burrowing animals. Rattlesnakes
always came out at night to hunt, causing him extra
concern. Happily, not a single snake could be found.
*When the country's too hard for a rattler to make a living, a
man's on the outskirts of Hell.*

He again crossed the railroad tracks, this time far
to the west, and silently made his way to where he was
close enough to the cabin to hear a murmuring of
voices from inside. Moving toward the shack in the
shadow of the huge water tank that imposed high
against the starry sky, he could soon make out what the
men inside were saying. *They were playing cards.*

Dallas edged his way alongside the unpainted planks
of the water station to where he could stealthily peek
through a window that was propped open to allow a
cooling breeze inside. Two bearded men sat at a
wooden table beneath a pair of coal-oil lamps that
hung from the ceiling. They were nonchalantly playing a game of euchre using matchsticks as chips. The
fact that Jasper Flatt had not killed these men was no
cause to relax. The outlaw could easily be hidden in

the shadows of that high water tower, as was Dallas, and using those railroad men as bait.

The bounty hunter was lowering himself from the window when the cold steel barrels of a shotgun poked hard into his neck.

"If you fancy your head staying on your shoulders, drop that rifle, hombre, and grab some sky," a gravelly voice intoned sternly.

Chapter 3

The bounty hunter kept a grip on his Sharps. "Frank, if you keep at being a railroad detective long enough, you'll eventually get lucky enough to happen onto a genuine outlaw and begin earning your paycheck."

The twin barrels of a ten-gauge shotgun left his neck to the sound of hammers being uncocked. "Dallas, what in the blue blazes are you doing spooking around in the middle of the night like the clumsiest Indian in Texas? We saw you coming a mile back, took you forever to sneak up this far."

"This has been a tiresome day. You fellows happen to have some coffee on?"

"Always. There's a train due through here about every six hours or so. The engineers appreciate a cup."

Dallas winced when a sudden gust of wind caused the tall wooden windmill that fed the tank to give out a squeak.

Frank Dutton chuckled. "Jumpy as you are, I'd go easy on the coffee."

"Being edgy can keep a person from getting shot."

"Yeah, I noticed," Frank said solemnly. "Now come on inside and meet the boys."

Joe Jenkins and Oscar Tillman, the men who were playing euchre, shook Dallas's hand and made his acquaintance.

"You make a success out of bounty hunting?" Oscar asked with obvious seriousness.

"So far," Dallas answered on his way to the coffeepot that set atop a small potbelly stove. In spite of the heat, a fire had to be kept burning to boil water or cook up a pot of beans. "Outlaws are generally a lot more inept than Frank here, which is a desirable trait."

"The fact that you're standing here is proof of that statement," the detective said. Frank Dutton wore his trademark natty black suit with a bow tie. He had paid rewards to Dallas for bringing in outlaws who were preying on railroad property over a dozen times. He also considered the bounty hunter to be a solid friend. "I reckon you're after that man who robbed the bank and killed the sheriff and those other fine folks in Fort Stockton."

Dallas finished pouring his coffee, then gave a puzzled look. "That just happened a few hours ago."

Frank grinned and motioned with his silver-cropped head to a brass telegraph key-set on an oak rolltop desk. "This is 1886. We have all of the modern conveniences these days. Every station of any railroad line of the Texas and New Orleans is equipped with a telegraphy set along with someone who can send and receive Morse code. There's no way anyone can outrun a cable." He hesitated. "Sorry to hear about Herb Perkins. He was a good lawman."

"So was the deputy." Dallas took a sip of what he considered to be the worst coffee he had ever tasted. "And the bank president left a widow with five little kids to raise."

Frank Dutton gave a sigh as he walked to stare out

the open window over the card table. "What is this fellow's name?"

"Jasper Flatt." Dallas forced down another swallow of the foul brew. He needed to stay alert. "Him and his brother Sam started out in the Indian territories robbing stages. Judge Parker isn't tolerant of such behavior and put a price on their heads. Then the Flatts moved south, robbing banks or travelers—those two aren't at all picky—killing at least four men that we know of. When they passed through San Angelo, my dad recognized them when they came in his saloon for a drink. I caught up with them the next day. That's when I put a hole in Sam. I've been in pursuit of Jasper ever since."

Dutton had been thumbing through a stack of papers on the desk while he listened. He stopped halfway through the pile and looked up. "Here's the dodger. I see those two are worth two thousand each. That's a mighty healthy reward; most outlaws aren't worth more than a few hundred bucks."

"The Flatts *enjoy* killing. That's what gave them value."

"You got one already?" Joe Jenkins, the telegraph operator, was in obvious awe. "Man, that's a fortune. I don't make a thousand dollars in an entire year."

Frank Dutton stared out into the night. "Dallas, the sheriff was already dead when you got to Fort Stockton, wasn't he?"

"Yeah, I was an hour behind Flatt."

"Then you didn't have any law to turn the body over to?" Dutton turned to his friend. "That means you've had to resort to desperate measures."

Dallas nodded. "Tomorrow will be the fourth day I've been packing Sam Flatt's head in a saddlebag. I had really hoped to be able to turn it over to

Sheriff Perkins. In this weather the thing is becoming pretty gamy."

Joe Jenkins's mouth dropped open in awe. "You cut an outlaw's head off and are packing it around with you?"

Frank shrugged. "What else was the man to do, for Pete's sake. Dallas has enough for an identification and he's not burdened with a lot of weight. Seems like a solid business practice to my way of thinking."

"I'll stick with being a telegraph operator," Joe said as he watched his decidedly pale friend, Oscar, run out the door headed for the outhouse.

"All I can offer is some salt and possibly a pound or so of stove ash," Frank said. "That ought to keep the smell down while not messing up his looks to the point of making him worthless."

Dallas glanced at the half-full cup of vile coffee and decided to leave it be. He wasn't *that* tired. "Obliged, but I was thinking you might take care of the matter, for a cut of the reward, of course."

"Can't help you any there." Frank clucked his tongue. "Not only would the president of the railroad get tolerable upset with me if the incident made the newspapers, but I'm under orders to stay put and check every train that comes through here for bums riding without a ticket. There's more folks than you'd believe jumping on when the train slows for a curve or when it's leaving town and ride for free. This type of thievery has to be dealt with."

"I'll appreciate the salt and ashes," Dallas said. "Then I need to be moving on."

"You can have Bob Morgan identify that head. He's an elected sheriff."

Dallas blinked in bafflement. "The last I heard, ol' Bob was the marshal of Bandera and has been since Wild Bill Hickok got himself plugged up in Deadwood."

Dutton smiled at the telegraph set. "You need to start keeping up on current events. Morgan's moved to that new silver-mining boomtown of Devil's Gate and gotten himself elected to sheriff. He's likely earning twice what he was in Bandera."

It was Dallas Handley's turn to cluck his tongue, "I've heard of Devil's Gate. The place is down near the border; supposedly there's some mighty rich mines being found." He thought for a moment. "I've got a deed to half interest in a claim down there, won it playing a game of poker. Might be worth something."

"Reckon you can check that out when you get there," Frank said.

"What do you mean *when* I get there. Jasper Flatt has got me a tad too occupied to go running off just for the fun of it."

Frank tapped a factory-made Three Kings cigarette from a pack and lit it on one of the coal-oil lamps. "About two hours before you showed up and began skulking round, a man leading a packhorse came riding down the road. He didn't bother us none and seemed to know where he was headed, so it never occurred to me he was worth a passel of money."

"Why didn't you tell me this earlier!" Dallas exclaimed. "I might have caught up with him by now."

"Simmer down, finish your coffee," Frank said calmly. "But first come over here, there's something you need to see."

Dallas joined the detective at the window.

"Notice that dark streak that cuts off to the south just past that third telegraph pole," Frank said.

Dallas blinked into the night. "Yeah, plain as the

nose on your face. It's a road that looks to wind toward those big steep mountains to the south."

"Yep," Dutton said, taking a puff on his cigarette sending a smoke ring to the ceiling. "The only place that road leads to is Devil's Gate. The country gets too rugged for anyone to get off it. Devil's Gate is where your boy went."

The bounty hunter gave a sigh, walked over, grabbed up the coffee, and chugged it down. "Leastwise he won't be a difficulty to track."

"That was my way of thinking," Frank said, laying his cigarette in a metal ashtray. "I'll fetch that salt now."

Chapter 4

The broken, jagged spires that sculpture the Chisos Mountains of the Big Bend area of West Texas lay before Dallas Handley in the bright light of morning like a string of medieval castles from some grim fairy tale.

Legend held that the word "Chisos" translates to "ghost" in a long-lost Apache dialect. Alsate, the last chief of the tribe that once inhabited this remote place, and his squaw, whose name has been lost to the ages, escaped from their white captors, who had killed all of their people save them. After a long chase in which both were badly wounded, they finally made their way home to die in their beloved mountains, the last of the Chisos Apache. When the wind blows through the jagged peaks, it makes a mournful sound. Some people claim it is the ghosts of Alsate and his wife, wailing over the sad fate of their people.

Dallas lit a fresh long nine cigar and studied the mountains. "I'd reckon ghosts would feel right at home up there," he said to no one. "Lots of peace and quiet without a passel of bothersome folks about."

Then he grew silent when he noticed a column of billowing black smoke drifting upward in the distance.

It came from the only low gap to be seen along the entire range of rugged mountains that stretched across the blue horizon as far as he could see.

"That smoke's probably from the mines at Devil's Gate, boilers for some sort of steam power most likely. I've also heard tell some sort of smelting is done to refine the ore." He took a long puff on his cigar and said, "Well, I'll learn what's there soon enough. If I can find Jasper Flatt and kill him before nightfall, I'll consider this to be a fine day."

Riding south on the wagon road that spiraled upward from the desert floor, Dallas was forced to move over several times to allow groups of Mexicans and their mule-drawn *carretas* to pass. The outgoing carts were empty; the returning ones were loaded high with scrub cedar, greasewood, mesquite, ocotillo, or even sagebrush. The only criteria for what they gathered seemed to be that it was able to burn.

Dallas noted the closer he got to the town of Devil's Gate, the more denuded the countryside. The Mexican wood gatherers had scoured the area for miles in all directions and, like a spreading cancer, were moving out even further, chopping down everything combustible and hauling it back to feed the insatiable maws of steam boilers. He wondered how long the sparse vegetation would last.

No matter. Those worries were for the mine owners. Then, Dallas remembered the deed to half interest in a claim to a mine in Devil's Gate that he had won only a couple of weeks ago. He had tucked the paper away in the small grip he had grabbed up to take along on this manhunt.

The stubble-bearded old prospector with black teeth

had been dead certain that his two pair would beat Dallas's hand. When the miner could not match a raise, he had tossed down a deed to a mine he claimed to be rich in silver and worth a fortune to anyone "who has enough sand in their craw to haul the ore out and live to spend any of the money."

Dallas had been holding four lucky ladies at the time, and therefore he did not overly concern himself with winning a claim. The three gold double eagles on the green baize were much more certain than half interest in some remote mine. However, now that he was already in the area of the mine, it would be something to check out once he had settled his business with the Flatt brothers. He pulled the brim of his hat low to shade his eyes from the bright morning sun that was quickly becoming relentless in a cloudless sky, and rode on in pursuit of a murderer.

The town of Devil's Gate could not have been more appropriately named, Dallas thought as he reined his horse to a stop on a low hill to survey his destination. Hard experience had taught him to never head into unfamiliar territory without first searching out handy places where sneaky outlaws could stage an ambush.

Devil's Gate was custom-made for evildoers. Boulders the size of wagons littered the entire canyon, having broken loose and tumbled down from tops of the red granite cliffs that stood sheer as a stone wall against the base of the tall mountains. The town itself was laid out in the flat of a canyon that formed the only passageway through the rugged peaks. On the other side would be the Rio Grande River and Mexico. A single man with a rifle stationed high in that imposing field of high rocks could hold off an army.

The silver mines were apparently confined to one lone rounded hill possibly a quarter mile from the steep mountain and conveniently situated just to the west of the town, providing an easy walk to and from the nearest saloons. Dallas noticed there had been only a few false-front wood structures erected. Most buildings were rude tents draped over flimsy frames, and had likely been put together in mere hours.

Studying the mines themselves, he noted there were only three shafts to be seen. Around two of the head frames, one on each side of the hill, he noticed abundant activity. The smallest mine, on the very summit between the two operating ones, seemed strangely inactive or abandoned. He surmised that the ore there must have given out.

The smoke he had noticed from miles back came from a low building that slanted to the small creek that meandered only a few thousand feet from the imposing mountains before the desert claimed the tiny stream to dry it completely. A single tall smokestack puffed out a continuous stream of dark fumes that hung tight to the valley, holding to the town like the embrace of the Grim Reaper.

"That place got well named," Dallas said to his horse. "If ever there was a doorway to the Devil's lair, I'm plain looking at it. The fact that Mexico isn't a far piece from downtown cinches the matter in my book."

Dallas gave a sigh and flicked the reins to start his horses on their way to the town where the thudding of the stamp mill, which was powered by a cloud-producing boiler, beat like growing thunder to echo against towering cliffs. It was akin to drumbeats for a firing squad.

When the bounty hunter rode into Devil's Gate, he felt the nape of his neck grow cold.

Chapter 5

A hanged man dangled from the crossbeam of a gallows at the very edge of Devil's Gate. Dallas noted that whoever the fellow was, he appeared to have been strung up some time ago. Birds had pecked his eyes out. Overhead, a dozen or so turkey vultures circled against a cloudless sky, drawn by the smell of death, while myriad flies buzzed about in the growing heat of another torrid day in the desert.

What few people who were out and about strangely seemed to ignore the grisly scene, never giving the gallows so much as a sideways glance.

"Must be a common occurrence hereabouts," Dallas mumbled. "Most towns I've been in, a hanging draws a crowd. Then folks have the decency to bury 'em. I can't figure Bob Morgan being so sloppy about matters such as this."

The hanged man was none of his affair. His business here needed to be taken care of quickly as possible so he could return to San Angelo and be among people who had more class than to leave a dead man dangling from a gallows at the head of the main street. Dallas lit a cigar to let the smoke clear out the stench from his lungs and rode on into Devil's Gate.

The most prominent building stood two stories high in the center of town. It had a sign across the front in flaming red letters announcing it to be DANTE'S INFERNO SALOON. Dallas looked up and down the cluttered valley that held as much garbage as it did structures, causing him to doubt anyone here had ever read any of Dante Alighieri's works, but he had to agree the name did seem appropriate to the surroundings.

He had been almost a week without a night's sleep. But Dallas had trained himself for such long treks as this one had become. When the trail traversed an area where ambush was unlikely, he slipped into a few restful moments of somnolence while still pushing ahead. If lucky enough to be able to stop for a meal, Dallas could catch as much as five minutes worth of sleep sitting upright in his chair. From an ancient Apache warrior, who swamped his father's saloon for beans and a room to stay in, he had learned the secrets of concentrating the mind. Adding in the beneficial effects of long nine cigars and coffee, he could stay on a manhunt for two weeks straight without spending a night in bed, and had.

Dallas pondered the possibility that Jasper Flatt had simply ridden through Devil's Gate and on to the relative safety of Mexico. Not that that move would alter the outcome. While a sheriff or Texas Ranger might be forced to stop at the border, Dallas would ignore it with impunity. What lawmen that could be found in Mexican border towns were usually glad to have gringo troublemakers removed from their midst without expense or effort on their parts.

No, Jasper Flatt is right here. The manner in which cold pinpricks played along the nape of his neck and worked their way down his spine was not to be denied. He raked his eyes up and down the street for any sign of the sheriff's office and came up blank. Wherever Bob Morgan had hung his shingle, it had to be on a side street. Then again, considering how new the place was—a year ago Devil's Gate did not exist—the sheriff might easily have been too busy dealing with crooks to letter a sign and hang it.

In any town the local saloon was always a good source of information. Saloons were the social centers where men met to talk about politics, the price of livestock, or simply to be among other people for a while. More than a few generally drank nothing stronger than coffee, hot chocolate, or sarsparilla.

Dallas dismounted and led his two horses to a water trough. After they had drunk their fill, he tied them to a hitching rail, then headed for Dante's Saloon. He hesitated a moment to check his Colt and add a cartridge to the cylinder. Keeping a live shell under the hammer when a man is carrying a pistol is not wise. Brushing against a limb or some similar accident could cause the handgun to fall, or the hammer might get struck in any manner, and the gun might fire with no regard as to where the slug would go. Heading for a possible gunfight, however, made adding one more cartridge to the cylinder a grand idea. It never ceased to amaze the bounty hunter just how much lead an outlaw could absorb and still keep breathing and shooting. Dallas doubted that Jasper Flatt would be inside the saloon, but if he was, getting their business settled before lunchtime would be agreeable.

The tinny harmony of an out-of-tune piano spilled from the batwing doors to clash with the distant rumble of the sprawling stamp mill and create an antithesis of sounds.

"All this place needs is a preacher to tell these pilgrims what's sinful and a pimp to sell it to them," Dallas mumbled as he sidled through the batwings to keep a slight profile while he sized up the crowd.

After a moment he realized Jasper Flatt wasn't among the fifteen or so souls who were inside at this hour of the morning. His quick scan had also disclosed that none of the patrons were drinking coffee and all were armed to the teeth with huge bowie knives. Dallas decided he had some learning to do when it came to mining camps. Devil's Gate was obviously a very tough town.

"What'll it be, stranger?" a chubby, bald barkeep asked in an oddly friendly and cheerful voice. "Just got a load of ice in yesterday, if'n you have a hankering for a cold mug of beer."

Dallas nodded, forced a thin smile, stepped up to the bar, and placed a boot on the brass rail. "It's a tad early for that. How about a hot cup of black coffee?"

The bartender snorted. "Can't do that, friend. The boss would have me out of here on my ear. He insists that anyone taking up space in here be a drinking man."

"Then I'll have that beer."

"Yes, sir, coming right up." The ponderous bartender fished the smallest mug Dallas had ever seen from an oak icebox and held it far below the tap so as to cause the beer to splash and leave a third of the glass as foam. "That'll be a dime. This is a pay-as-you-go joint."

Dallas laid a silver dollar on the bar, having to remind himself that freight to this remote place must be atrocious; every saloon in Texas charged a nickel for a beer. "You can keep the change for some information."

The bartender's eyes narrowed; then he snatched the coin and stuck it into a pocket of his filthy apron. "Ask away. And for a tip like that you can even call me Harry."

Dallas swirled the beer around and took a sip. There wasn't much more than a couple of healthy swallows in the mug, but he had to admit that it was cold. "I'm looking for the sheriff's office."

Three burly men standing next to him grew silent. Harry shrugged his shoulders. "Sure, two blocks south, then right to the middle building. There ain't no sign 'cept on the door, but you can't mistake the place when you see it, an' Sinker's generally there this time of day."

"Sinker?" Dallas asked with a raised eyebrow.

"Yep," Harry said, "Sinker Wilson does a right fine job of keeping law and order, he does for sure."

Dallas set down the empty mug. "I was informed Bob Morgan came down here from Bandera and took the job of sheriff."

The rough-looking bearded man next to Dallas turned to him. "That's a fact, but he didn't last. Got himself shot right behind the jail when he went to the outhouse. Never did figure out who done it."

Harry spoke up. "Now mister, don't you go thinking this ain't a peaceful town. Sinker runs a tight ship, he does for sure."

"I saw a reminder to behave on the way in," Dallas said.

"Bad feller that Don Ruggles," Harry said after swatting a fly. "Raped a nice pretty little saloon girl, he did. Sinker believes in leaving lessons hang around for a spell. Says it causes folks to respect the law."

The bearded man next to Dallas tossed back a shot of whiskey and muttered, "Ruggles was up in that cabin of his at the mine the night that so-called rape happened." His voice became lower. "And how does a man come to rape a whore anyway?"

Harry glared at the drunk. "You'll keep your yap shut if you know what's good for you, Arnie. Poxon doesn't like folks talkin' bad about Devil's Gate and spreading rumors."

"Yeah," Arnie snorted, "that gallows out there provides a mighty warm feeling that folks can admire." He banged his shot glass on the bar. "Gimme another."

"Only if you'll stop shooting your mouth off," the bartender said, turning to grab a bottle of Bear's Breath Whiskey. "Tiberius Poxon pays darn good money to his men, and besides, this place wouldn't even be here if he hadn't bought up all those little claims. These days it takes a big mine with a mill to make a profit. I'd reckon he has a right to run this town any way he dad-gum pleases."

"Poxon ain't got the Forlorn Hope Mine yet," Arnie said. "Ruggles only had half interest. That partner of his, Ike, had sense enough to hightail it out of here for a healthier climate. That mine's smack dab on the mother lode and is richer than sin. Poxon's got a powerful hankering to own it."

Dallas cocked his head in thought, finished the last swallow of beer, and slid the empty mug across the bar. "Thanks for the directions," he said, then headed out the batwing doors without another word.

Before untying the horses, Dallas took a moment to surreptitiously open a saddlebag and fish out the deed to the half interest to the mine he had won near here. There was something about the name of it that had caused a flicker of recollection. Dallas also had listened closely enough to the conversation in the saloon to realize idle talk in Devil's Gate could be fatal.

Hunkering over to shelter his actions from prying eyes, he unfolded the deed. Dallas Handley gave a hard swallow and quickly stowed the paper inside his vest. He had gotten the deed from a fellow by the name Ike McKenna, but as he had suspected, the name of the mine he now had a half interest in was the same claim the hanged man had owned the other half of, the Forlorn Hope.

Chapter 6

As Dallas led horses up the main street heading for the sheriff's office, he deliberately moved slow, sizing up the town. There was only the one saloon, which was odd. A sprawling clapboard hotel called the Worthington advertised itself as being "a slice of Heaven in Devil's Gate." A voluptuous girl standing in an upstairs window wearing a low-cut dress indicated that the hotel did not rely solely on tourists for its income.

He noted the usual dry-goods and hardware stores, two barbershops, a livery stable, a dentist's office, along with the customary undertaker's parlor. From high above town to the west, on a flat mesa at the base of the steep mountains, an imposing white three-story mansion of a home overlooked both the town and the mines from a lofty perch.

A leathery-faced old Mexican with long white hair, who was struggling under the weight of a gunnysack full of melons, noticed Dallas staring at the imposing house and spoke to him in Spanish. "*Perdón, señor,* I have not seen you here before. But I see you looking at the home of Señor Tiberius Poxon. He own all of the rich mines and is the *jefe* of this town."

Dallas nodded and answered in the Mexican's native tongue. Nearly everyone who lived long in Texas learned to speak at least passable Spanish. "*Gracias, amigo.* I am just passing through. When I have taken care of a matter, then settled some business I have with the sheriff, I'll be on my way."

"Señor." The Mexican's eyes widened with fear as he crossed himself with his free hand. "May Dios be with you when you go to the sheriff." The old man hoisted the sack of melons and scurried off in the direction of a grocery store.

Cheerful place, Dallas thought. *I've attended funerals where folks had a sunnier disposition than hereabouts. Leaving a man hanging from a gallows in the middle of the street would account for a somber disposition, I suppose.*

Dallas gave one last scan to check for Jasper Flatt, then tied the horses and made the short walk to visit with Sheriff Wilson. He hoped the man was an elected sheriff, or had at least been legally appointed to the job. Only a recognized officer of the law was authorized to pay out money for rewards. The lawmen never gave over the cash. Once the identity of the outlaw had been established, the officer would issue a voucher that could be cashed at any bank. After sizing up Devil's Gate, Dallas decided he would wait until he got home to San Angelo before tempting any of the locals by carrying cash. Outlaws were plentiful enough without enticing new ones to take up the occupation.

The sheriff's office came as such a surprise, Dallas stopped to puff on his cigar and look it over. The long, low structure was constructed with some of the most massive stonework he had ever seen. A few tiny barred windows in the rear of the building showed it also contained an attached jail, which was not uncommon. What took the bounty hunter aback were the pair of massive wooden doors hinged at the top and held open with chains displaying the threatening dark maws of cannons. From his small experience with field pieces gained from visiting Army forts, he knew they were six-pounders. A most formidable weapon, and one totally unexpected to be found guarding a jail in a remote mining town.

Probably the Lipan Apache have become a threat, Dallas thought. *There is no reason outside of holding off a tribe of wild Indians to justify turning a jail into a fort like they've done here.*

Dallas gave a dismissive shrug, tossed the stub of his long nine to the dry dirt, ground it out with the heel of his boot, then headed for a visit with the sheriff of Devil's Gate.

The door was built of *fierro madera*, a heavy hardwood that the gringos called ironwood, laced together with massive steel straps and hung on hinges heavy enough to have weighed at least one hundred pounds each. No bank in Texas had such an imposing or bulletproof entranceway. It amazed Dallas that it swung open as easily as it did without the expected squeak. Then he quit admiring the architecture to focus on a fat man with deep-set pig eyes setting behind a desk pointing the twin barrels of a shotgun square at his middle.

"Howdy, stranger," the corpulent man with the gun said cheerfully. "With you being new to our town and all, I reckon you didn't know there was a law against carrying a gun in the city limits. The fine's five bucks. Pay up."

Dallas fought to control his growing anger. He decided that letting his true feelings come to light might damage his chances of turning over a two-thousand-dollar head. "Sheriff Wilson, I presume. My name is Dallas Handley. I'm a bounty hunter and was a friend of Bob Morgan, who you took over from, I believe."

The imposing shotgun did not waver as the fat man said, "I'm Sinker Wilson an' if your friend Morgan had been careful like me, he'd still be sitting in this chair instead of pushing up cactus in the cemetery. But you being a bounty hunter changes things. You need to register your guns. The fee is ten dollars for that."

Dallas swallowed hard and waited a moment to compose himself. In all of his years of bounty hunting he had dealt with some really unlikable lawmen, but none of them ever made him have to force down the urge to shoot him as Sinker Wilson had managed to do. Taking care to move slowly, he reached into his pocket, took out a gold eagle, then stepped to the desk and dropped it in front of the sheriff.

Sinker Wilson leaned the sawed-off shotgun on an open drawer, grabbed up the coin, and gave a nod. "I can see you're a man of the law. Always happy to help out folks that keep outlaws thinned out."

"Glad to hear that, Sheriff." Dallas spoke slowly, carefully choosing his words. "I assume you are duly authorized to give vouchers as payment for wanted men."

Wilson gave a snort. "Hell, yes. Tiberius Poxon himself gave me this job an' he's friends of the governor along with a whole passel of Austin politicians. If you've got anyone that needs turning in, bring 'em on. I don't want it said Devil's Gate ain't a tough town on lawbreakers."

"I noticed evidence of that when I rode in."

"Fellow hangin' out there's a rapist. Can't abide a man that'll do that to a woman."

"I didn't know that was a hanging offense in Texas."

"It is if the mayor an' Poxon say so."

Dallas decided to get on with business. "I brought in a man wanted for murder among other crimes. Fellow's got a two-thousand-dollar price on his head, which, since I'm in pursuit of his brother, that was all I was able to bring along for identification."

Sinker Wilson grabbed up a bottle of whiskey from the floor, took a healthy drink, then corked it and set it on the cluttered desk. "Well, fetch the damn thing. I always need a shot to brace me for times like these."

Without hesitation Dallas spun and strode outside. He wanted to get this matter over with as quickly as possible. The sheriff was one small step above the type of man he went after for reward money, possibly even worse. There was no doubt Sinker Wilson was corrupt. And corrupt men were never to be trusted.

When he came to where the horses were tied, Dallas took a canvas sack from a bedroll and shook it open. Then he quickly fished out Sam Flatt's head and stuck it into the bag. Women and some of the more sensitive citizens had a tendency to be squeamish in matters such as this. A little discretion on his part often made life simpler. Once, in the town of Wichita Falls, the wife of a Baptist preacher had become hysterical over him packing a head down a street just to claim his bounty. That incident had cost him five dollars for the local doctor to sedate the screaming lady. There had already been enough added expense without taking any unnecessary chances. He twisted the sack closed and headed back to the strangely fortified sheriff's office.

The chubby Sinker Wilson apparently had not moved during Dallas's absence, yet the whiskey bottle had been lowered by a good three fingers.

"Well, bring it out an' let's get on with it," the sheriff grumbled.

"The head belongs to Sam Flatt. I also have a copy of the wanted poster."

Sinker Wilson's dark eyes narrowed to anthracite pinpoints. He gave a grunt as he stood to take the sack.

A moment later he held the head high, grasping it by a handful of greasy black, salt-encrusted hair.

"Hell, this messy thing could belong to anybody. For all I know you might have dug it up in the cemetery."

Before Dallas could say a word, Sinker had turned and stepped back to a potbelly stove with a pot of coffee boiling on top. Instantly the sheriff opened the door and tossed Sam Flatt's head into the inferno. "Reckon this ain't gonna be a payday, bounty hunter."

Dallas fought a building red rage. The piggish lawman had just cost him two thousand dollars. "I didn't expect a sheriff to do something like that. I've been turning in outlaws for a lot of years. Hell's bells, man, you didn't even look at the picture on the poster."

"Saw enough to know it weren't him." Sinker Wilson ran a finger idly along a scar on his cheek. "Count your blessings, bounty hunter, that I don't toss you in jail for attempting to defraud an officer of the law. Now get out of my office."

Dallas felt his gun hand twitch, but the man *was* a sheriff. Shooting him would only cause more problems. And there was one more outlaw in Devil's Gate worth a pile of money. Jasper Flatt he would have to pack away to another, more honest town no matter how difficult the task. Any further business with Sinker Wilson was something to avoid.

Without another word the bounty hunter spun and strode outside. Now he realized why those cannon were in place. It was more than likely that a great many people wanted to be rid of this sheriff. Then a thin grin crossed his lips. *Maybe there will be a price on Sinker Wilson's head someday soon.*

Buoyed by the good thought, Dallas decided to get a room in the hotel, have a good meal, a bath, and shave. It would be a delight to sleep in a bed for a change.

Jasper Flatt was here, without a doubt. No person of his caliber would be in any hurry to leave such a charming town as the aptly named Devil's Gate. Besides that cheering thought, Dallas also now knew he owned half interest in a rich silver mine. The problem with that was staying alive once the fact became known.

Chapter 7

"Welcome to the Worthington Hotel." The scarecrow-thin clerk with a droopy mustache hesitated to catch his breath, a certain sign of a lunger. "The hotel rooms with board are three dollars." He gave a gasp. "Lulu's rooming house costs two. Pay here an' get a check good for an hour. There's five mighty pretty girls to choose from."

"I'll just take the hotel room." Dallas was mildly surprised to find a brass-check system in such a small town. In the larger cities buying a chip to give the girl was commonplace. Most men agreed this arrangement kept the soiled doves generally more trustworthy, with the added benefit of allowing the man to know the cost of the ladies' services ahead of time.

"I'm on duty until ten tonight if you change your mind."

"A bath, a good meal, and a barber will be all I'm in need of," Dallas said.

"You a mining man?" the clerk asked, lighting a cigarette.

"No," Dallas answered, realizing that in this town a

wrong word could get a person killed. "I'm just passing through."

"Take a good look around. Devil's Gate is bigger than New York City."

Dallas cocked his head in obvious puzzlement.

The clerk blew a smoke ring and cackled. "Well, it ain't all been built just yet."

"I suppose the rich mines are what everyone's counting on."

"No other reason to be here 'cept to get rich."

Talkative as the sickly man was, Dallas decided to visit for a few minutes to see what he could learn about the town. "I heard tell a man by the name of Poxon owns all of the mines."

"Tiberius Poxon got mighty lucky. He's richer than Croesus these days, has a manager named Harry Latts to handle problems." The clerk suffered a long coughing spell. He took a sip from a pewter pocket flask and continued. "Poxon owns most every business too, the saloon an' even this place."

Dallas gave a nod. None of this came as any surprise.

"But I'm betting there's a lot of other silver veins out there that ain't been found," the clerk said. He took another sip of whiskey. "When I get a day off, I'm out prospecting."

"I hope you strike it rich. Tell me, why does the sheriff let a body hang from the gallows? To my way of thinking, that's not a great way to boom a town."

"Sinker Wilson has his own way of doing things. That feller they hung raped a gal who works upstairs. Can't figger why he just didn't pay her; the outcome would have been better for him. But to answer your question, Sinker says that man will stay there until he rots as a reminder for folks to behave themselves."

The long speech winded the consumptive. Dallas

waited a while before saying, "I heard a fellow by the name of Bob Morgan was the sheriff."

"Was until three months ago. Nice fellow that Morgan. Went out back to get firewood one day and got shot so full of holes they could have rented him out for a screen door. Never did figger out who did it."

"The jail looks like a fort."

"Sinker done all that. Says he don't plan on taking chances with his health. Did you know he put in some cannons?"

"I saw them."

"They're from the war. Poxon bought 'em cheap. Sinker loaded 'em with steel chains instead of balls. I hear a chain'll spin all around kind of crazylike an' chop anyone it hits clear in two."

"I hope there's never any need to find out."

"Amen to that, but if someone ever tries to break anyone out of jail or generally acts up, Sinker sure won't hesitate to shoot the things at 'em."

"It's a comfort to be in such a law-abiding town. I'll be getting to that bath now."

The clerk wheezed. "Tub's down at the end of the hall. Hot water's a dime extra, but it ain't worth the cost. Regular water comes out of the pipe hot enough to boil eggs in."

"Sounds like the name Devil's Gate fits right well."

"Rich mines ain't found in easy country."

Dallas nodded, then turned and walked down the hallway to his room. He inserted the skeleton key that was attached to a large metal disk with the number twelve stamped on it into the lock and swung the door wide. The room was surprisingly neat and clean. A brass bed set next to an oak dresser. There was a night table that held a crystal pitcher along with four glasses. A lone window was framed by white-lace curtains. He thought about opening the window to let in fresh air, but the myriad of greenflies buzzing about outside caused him to choose stale air over a roomful of flies.

After a long, leisurely bath he felt ready to find a barber for a trim and shave, then enjoy a decent restaurant. The consumptive clerk had been correct about not needing hot water. His skin was still beet red from his soak. Dallas took the crystal pitcher and filled it with water before leaving. By the time he returned, it might be cooled down enough to drink.

When he left his room, a door across the hallway cracked open. A pair of dark eyes framed in blue flickered for a brief second; then the door slammed closed and he heard the harsh metallic sound of a bolt being slid home. When he walked past he noticed a small, neatly handwritten sign on the door: VELVET DAWN. Dallas now knew the working name of one of the girls who practiced the oldest profession in the Worthington Hotel. The brief encounter also told him one other thing. There had been an unmistakable flash of fear in those wide doe eyes. From the way the town of Devil's Gate was shaping up, he could easily understand her trepidation.

In contrast to the hotel clerk, the taciturn tonsorial artist who trimmed his hair, and gave him a couple of painful nicks from a straight razor during a shave, had kept quiet as the proverbial stone. The shaky old silver-haired barber had charged a dollar for his doubtful services. Dallas was coming to the opinion that it did not pay to ask what anything cost in this town. It would be simpler and save time to just extend a handful of money and let them take what they wanted. A few of his manhunts had taken him to booming cattle towns such as Dodge City and Abilene. Those places were downright bargains to visit compared to Devil's Gate.

When he stepped into the street, Dallas took a moment to consider the pall that had fallen over Devil's Gate like a shroud. A burning sensation in his eyes and throat told him that thick smoke from the mine boilers along with clouds of dust from the thudding stamp mill were being jammed into the narrow canyon by a breeze from the north. This was not an uncommon direction for the wind to blow in Texas. Dallas blinked his watery eyes and decided he had another good reason to dislike the place. Anyone living here for long would certainly suffer permanent damage. The consumptive clerk at the hotel would be lucky to make it here a year, breathing air thick enough with soot and grit to blot out the sun.

It's time to ferret out Jasper Flatt, drape his body over my packhorse, and head for a better climate, Dallas thought as he headed for a restaurant. *I can hire a mining engineer to come and check out that silver mine once I'm back in a civilized town.*

Dallas felt fairly certain that his interest in the Forlorn Hope claim was valuable, possibly worth more than Sam Flatt's head should have been. One thing he knew without doubt: If word got bandied about Devil's Gate that he owned a coveted piece of a rich mine here, he would be troubled with all sorts of people wanting to either shoot or hang him. He could well understand the barber keeping his mouth shut about even the weather.

A deep rumble of complaint from his stomach told him a decent meal was in order. There was a restaurant inside the hotel, but for some reason he could not put a finger on, he decided to try another eatery. Perhaps, Dallas mused as he strode along the boardwalk, blinking his eyes to clear away the burning sensation, it was because the hotel was owned by the same man that seemed to own the town. He had yet to meet Tiberius Poxon and had no plans to do so. But the cold pricking sensation that came to the back of his neck whenever the man's name was mentioned was a warning omen that it probably wouldn't be wise to ignore.

Next to the undertaker's parlor, a sign over an unpainted door advertised the SILVER BARON CHOP HOUSE. Dallas gave a cough to clear his lungs of acrid smoke and went inside. There were maybe a dozen clients that were congregated where two tables had been placed together. The group, all men, grew silent and scrutinized him carefully while he hung his gray felt hat on a peg and took a seat at a vacant table to the rear of the building. Dallas noticed every eye focused on his sidearm. Then it struck him that he had paid Sheriff Wilson a gold eagle to gain his permission to pack a gun.

In the past few years quite a number of towns had passed ordinances against carrying guns. Dallas had not noticed any shortage of outlaws due to these laws. It seemed to him that they only served to deprive the good citizens of the means to defend themselves and their town from evildoers who certainly never checked their guns in with the local marshal. He gave a slight shrug and decided the lawmakers would come to their senses someday.

A plump, flaxen-haired woman, with her hair drawn back into a tight bun and with a lit cigarette dangling from her mouth, came shuffling from a side door and plopped a menu in front of him without uttering a single word. He had already decided it would be a wise move to order a meal that might not cause problems later.

"I'll have a plate of bacon with some fried potatoes and a couple of eggs." He hesitated a brief moment. "Well cooked, with a cup of black coffee."

"Takes a few minutes, I'll fetch your coffee while you

wait," the woman mumbled, spun, and stomped off to the kitchen.

Dallas noticed the group of men near the front of the restaurant were still staring at him. He gave an agreeable nod. "Howdy, fellows."

To a man, they all stood, grabbed their hats, and went out the front door; not a single one had even acknowledged his attempt at being congenial.

A person could say folks here in Devil's Gate are consistent at least, Dallas thought. *I haven't met a nice one yet.*

The waitress brought him a cup of tepid coffee, spilling some when she slammed it on the table, then returned several minutes later carrying a chipped plate that held a few strips of blackened bacon alongside a small heap of potatoes that were raw enough Dallas decided they might sprout if someone planted them.

"Ain't got no eggs," the waitress grumbled, causing ashes from her cigarette to fall on the bacon. "That'll be a dollar for the grub an' another quarter for the coffee."

Dallas smiled, fished a pair of sliver dollars from his pocket, and tossed them on the wooden table to ring like a bell. "Great-looking meal, ma'am. Y'all keep the change for your good service and sparkling disposition."

The woman gave a grunt, scooped up the coins, and stomped off, the boards squeaking from her weight.

He sighed, grabbed up the salt shaker, and dusted the potatoes. On manhunts he had on occasion been forced to choke down some rather unpalatable victuals. This meal, however, resembled something that had been fished from out of a campfire. He made a vow to eat at the hotel the next time, then began pecking at the portions of his food that appeared edible.

When he stepped back out onto the boardwalk, the smoke and soot in the air seemed to be even heavier than before. What he had been able to consume of his meal began to weigh on his stomach. Dallas realized that it had been days since he had had a decent night's sleep.

"Jasper Flatt can wait until morning for his killing," he mumbled. "I'll be rested then, and hopefully the weather will be more agreeable."

As he walked back to his hotel room while keeping his eyes peeled for the wanted man, Dallas observed that while it was only late afternoon, a few coal-oil lamps could be seen burning in windows, so dense was the pollution from the mining operation.

When he came to the door to his room, he noticed it to be slightly ajar. He remembered clearly that he had locked it when he left. Pulling out his Peacemaker, Dallas stood to one side and swung the door wide. A quick glance inside caused him to relax.

"Please, sir, come in quickly and close the door," the dark-haired girl sitting on his bed pleaded.

Dallas nodded agreeably and did as the lovely lady asked.

Chapter 8

"I must say that this is the most agreeable thing to happen to me since I hit this jerkwater town." Dallas Handley scanned the room before returning his Colt to its holster. More than a few men had been distracted by situations like this only to wake up with a lump on their head and their wallet missing.

"I'm sorry to have to impose on you like this," the girl said.

Her wide, dark doelike eyes were the same ones he had seen peeking at him earlier. The fear was still there too. Dallas noted the favorable way the girl filled out the tight red-print dress she wore, her ample breasts straining to be free. The young lady had silky sable hair that cascaded down her narrow shoulders like a waterfall at midnight. Her high cheekbones and dusky skin spoke of distant Indian ancestry. He thought she was one of the most stunningly beautiful girls he had ever set eyes on.

"You're the girl from the room down the hall, the one who watched me when I left," Dallas said. "Velvet Dawn I believe is the name."

"That's my working name, sir. My given name is

Constance MacDougal. I came here from New Orleans to try and make enough money in a mining town to get out of this business, but this is a terrible place."

Dallas grinned. "You must have eaten in the Silver Baron too." Then his face grew serious. "Ma'am, I can appreciate you might be having problems here, I really can. Only I'm plumb tuckered out from a lot of hard days in the saddle. Maybe later on when I've gotten some sleep, I might come and knock on your door."

"Please, sir, I'm not here for money. I see you are carrying a gun. I thought you might be a lawman. No one else in Devil's Gate is allowed a gun."

"No, ma'am." Dallas watched the girl's face and saw her spirits sink. "I'm not."

"I was so in hopes."

"My name is Dallas Handley from San Angelo, Texas. I make my living as a bounty hunter. I'm here on a manhunt for a murderer. When I settle with him, I'll be on my way. Tell me, why would a pretty little thing like you be hoping to run into a lawman?"

Velvet Dawn had been sitting on the side of the bed. She stood, straightened her dress, and shook out her raven hair. When she came to face him, Dallas realized just how short and tiny she was, possibly not five feet tall, one hundred pounds at the most. The fear in her eyes had turned into mirrors of defeat.

"Because, Mr. Handley, if I do not get out of Devil's Gate, Tiberius Poxon will have me killed."

Dallas cocked his head. He did not doubt the girl was being truthful. "Sit back down on the bed and tell me about it. *All* about what is going on here. Then, I'll see what I might be able to do to help you out."

"I came to this town a few months ago, not too long after the silver strikes were made. As I told you, I came here only to make a lot of money. I make no apologies for what I am, Mr. Handley. A girl on her own has very few options."

"You can call me Dallas, ma'am, and I'm about as far from a prude that you'll ever run across. Go ahead and tell me why this Poxon fellow is going to kill you."

"And I prefer being called Velvet. That name is a lot softer than Constance. But to answer your question, I need to give you a little background on the town."

"I've already gathered Tiberius Poxon owns most all of the mines and controls the town."

Velvet Dawn gave a sigh and stared out the window at the dull red glow of a lowering sun that was all but masked by dark clouds of smoke. "Anyone coming to Devil's Gate to do business deals with Poxon. They either pay exorbitant cuts as blackmail—the city calls them taxes—or they work directly for him."

"And those who disagree with this?"

"Accidents are common. Then, there is always the sheriff and his deputies to arrest people on trumped-up charges. Those folks are always found guilty of a hanging offense or get shot attempting a 'jail break.'"

Dallas took a pack of cigarettes from a vest pocket, tapped a couple out, and offered one to the girl. She smiled as he lit both of their cigarettes with one lucifer. It was the first time he had seen hope on her pretty face.

"I think Tiberius Poxon needs a visit from the Texas Rangers," Dallas said. "Even rich men have to live by the law."

"Not him. Poxon has a manager, Harry Latts, to keep the town under his thumb. Sheriff Wilson and his deputy, Garrick Sparks, do what they are told. No one is willing to go up against him, not after what happened the last time."

Dallas took a puff on his cigarette. "Tell me about it."

"A few business owners banded together. They

elected a mayor who sent for an honest sheriff to clean up the town."

"That sheriff must have been Bob Morgan. I was told he came here. He was a good man."

"Sheriff Morgan hadn't been here a week when he got killed after he went out back of the jail to gather up some wood for the stove. I heard he was shot over a dozen times. Then the mayor was found hanging from a beam in the livery stable. Of course the sheriff called it suicide. Now, even the mayor is nothing but a puppet for Poxon. His grip on this town is one of iron."

"I gathered that much already," Dallas said. "I think now you need to tell me why he wants you dead."

Velvet Dawn's lower lip began to quiver as her smile fled. "I was forced to testify in court against a man . . . claim he raped me. I had never even set eyes on him before. I didn't want to do it, but Sinker Wilson made me."

Dallas watched as Velvet pulled off a house slipper to show angry red swollen toes.

"The sheriff and deputy tied me to the bed. Then Sinker came with needles and a hammer. He drove those needles under every toenail on my left foot before saying a word. Then he sneered at me and said he would do the same thing to my other foot if I didn't do what I was told." She began sobbing. "They hung that poor man on my say-so. And I'm the only one who knows the truth of the matter. Poxon won't be safe as long as I'm alive; he *has* to make sure the truth never comes out."

"I take it the fellow I saw hanging from the gallows when I rode in was the man who got convicted."

"Yes," she sobbed. "His name was Don Ruggles. Everyone knows he was killed so Poxon could get his hands on the Forlorn Hope Mine. That is the only rich vein he doesn't already own. Harry Latts claimed that Ruggles owed him money. The judge gave him the deed as payment, but Tiberius Poxon now owns it."

"I heard Ruggles only had a half interest in the claim."

"That's true, but I heard them say that if the other owner doesn't show up by the first of September to do . . . I think it's called assessment work . . . the interest is forfeited."

"And if he does show up, he'll meet with a fatal accident."

"That is how Poxon does business and now you know why I have to leave here."

"Yeah, and I'm developing a real dislike for this Poxon and I've yet to meet him."

"He's not what you would expect. I'd guess him to be in his forties, his hair is mostly silver. The man is nothing but muscle, not an ounce of fat. He doesn't drink or smoke. By all accounts he's never been seen with a woman, just stays mostly up at the big house of his while pulling strings and having Harry Latts take care of business."

"Speaking of business, once I've settled with Jasper Flatt, I'll be heading out. I'll be right happy to take you along. Do you have a horse? I'll have a body draped over my extra."

Velvet Dawn's eyes widened. "This Jasper Flatt's got a brother named Sam?"

Dallas gave a nod. "Used to have." He decided to spare the young lady all of the details. "I settled his hash just outside of San Angelo. Jasper I've followed to this delightful place." He cocked an eyebrow. "How do you know about the Flatt brothers?"

"Their father lives here. Jack Flatt runs the livery stable."

"That explains why Jasper hightailed it to Devil's Gate."

"He doesn't have much to concern him here."

Dallas tapped out a couple of fresh cigarettes from the pack. "Why's that?"

"Jack is one of Poxon's boys, and there's one more thing you should know."

"Go ahead and tell me. The way this town's shaping up nothing will surprise me."

Velvet Dawn turned to him. "Jack Flatt is the mayor of Devil's Gate."

Icy pinpricks began working their way down his spine. "Now *that* did come as a surprise. I reckon now I can't just walk up and shoot Jasper Flatt like I was planning to do. The problem is, I've already met with Sinker Wilson and he knows why I'm here. I'd venture this situation is getting somewhat treacherous."

"Dallas," she said, "I honestly believe you are in more danger than I am. These are really bad men."

"Jasper Flatt has murdered a lot of people. He has a two-thousand-dollar reward on his head and I intend to collect it. His daddy being the mayor does sort of muddy the water, however. I'll be forced to study on the situation, that's for certain."

"Please, Dallas, let's just ride away from here. I'm *so* afraid."

"Bounty hunting is a testy business. I've run up against some tough hombres before, but I can't recall such a collection of them as this place has. And it just occurred to me that my horses are stabled at Jack Flatt's livery stable."

"We could leave on the stage together. Even Sinker Wilson wouldn't be stupid enough to try anything when the Overland coach is here."

"I'll give the matter some thought, but I'm plumb

tuckered out. Maybe I'll come up with an idea or two once I've caught some sleep."

Velvet Dawn looked at him with pleading eyes. "Please give me ten dollars to hand over to Link. They took all of my money. If I turn that much in and tell him it's for all night, I can stay here with you."

Dallas fished an eagle from his pocket. "You stay off that foot. This Link fellow, he's the lunger who clerks?"

"Yes, he runs both the hotel and the girls for Poxon."

"I'll be right back." He gave her a reassuring smile. "A sawbuck to keep you safe will be the best money I'll have spent in this damn town."

Chapter 9

Cheerful red rays from a flowering sunrise shooting through the window showed that a change of wind direction had scoured all of the smoke from the craggy canyon. Its stark beauty was lost on the couple in the second-story room of the Worthington Hotel. They lay together in bed, propped up on feather pillows, smoking cigarettes and discussing their chances of getting out of Devil's Gate alive.

Velvet Dawn flicked a playful finger about Dallas's ear. "I'm glad to see you're no longer too tuckered out. A girl forgets what it's like having a man actually make love to her with kindness and caring."

"You're a nice lady, Velvet. I'm only sorry I couldn't have helped you out before Sinker Wilson hurt you like he did." Dallas took a puff on his cigarette, his features growing coarse. "I do intend to express my displeasure with that man, but I'm having difficulty deciding how to shoot a sheriff and make it come across as a good idea. Generally, actions like that are frowned on."

"Let's just leave Devil's Gate. If we don't . . . and quick . . . I honestly believe Poxon will order us both killed."

Dallas thought for a long minute before answering

her. "After finding out the Flatt brothers are the mayor's sons, along with the fact that I've already killed one of them, I'm of the opinion you're most likely right."

"The Overland stage comes in about noon. If we show up about then, saddle our horses, and leave with the stage, I don't think even Sinker Wilson would be stupid, or desperate, enough to try and stop us."

"From what I know of the sheriff, he'd need to ask Tiberius Poxon for permission before getting a haircut."

"You're right about that. All we need to buy is a few minutes. Sinker won't have time to act unless he's a lot quicker thinker than anyone has good reason to suspect."

Dallas rolled over to the nightstand, grabbed up his pocket watch, and flipped open the case. "The stage won't be due for quite a spell, darlin'. I'm wondering what *can* we do to pass all of that time."

"I've got a deck of cards in my room," Velvet Dawn said teasingly.

"I'm sure you do," Dallas said turning to the smiling, raven-haired beauty. "But I once promised a preacher I would give up gambling." Then he kissed her ruby lips and drew her to him.

When the Overland stage came creaking down the dusty main street of Devil's Gate, Dallas and Velvet Dawn slipped quickly from the front door of the hotel. They mixed with the growing crowd that came to greet the stage, while working their way toward the livery stable.

"Dang it all," the scruffy jehu complained as he climbed down from the driver's seat. "I never seen the likes of a town that'd leave a body danglin' from a gallows as a greetin' for folks. Not only is it plumb spooky, the smell's getting worse every time I make this run."

Vernon Camper, the station agent and telegrapher,

met the driver with a sack of mail. "The sheriff thinks it's a good idea to let folks know the law hereabouts isn't to be trifled with."

"You can tell ole Sinker that the message seems to have took better than he wants. There ain't a soul coming in on the stage. Same as yesterday." He gave a head shake to the burly shotgun guard atop the stage, who was leaning against the driver's seat snoring up a storm. "An' the bad men have been ignoring us to the point that Wesley's bored near to death."

While a few merchants were picking up items the stagecoach had brought in, Dallas and Velvet Dawn used the distraction to move along the fronts of buildings until they came to the entranceway of the livery and stepped inside the shadowy building.

"I'm here for my horses," Dallas said to the man standing behind a long counter who had his back to him.

When the hostler spun to him, Dallas stared into the startled face of Jasper Flatt.

"Holy shit," the outlaw sputtered as his eyes widened while his hand reached for the Navy pistol at his side.

"Ah, dammit," Dallas grumbled as he flicked out his Peacemaker. A slug of hot lead struck the outlaw square in the chest, blowing him backward in a spray of crimson before he was able to clear leather.

"I *did* mention his daddy ran this joint," Velvet Dawn commented.

"I remember, but being worth what he was dead, I'd figured on Jasper having enough smarts to not be out dealing with the public."

"This *is* Devil's Gate."

"And I was of the opinion this idiot wouldn't show up and cost us a nice quiet ride out of here. Let's get those horses saddled. A quick run for it still might get us past Sinker Wilson."

Velvet surprised him by grabbing up a saddle as if it were light as a feather. "Then quit jawing and get on with it. Leaving this place gets to be a better idea every minute."

Dallas was cinching the saddle on his horse when the ominous sound of hammers being clicked back on a shotgun caused him to freeze.

"Put them hands high and keep 'em there, bounty hunter, and you'll live long enough to hang." Sinker Wilson's gravely voice echoed inside the huge livery building like water dripping inside of a tomb.

"Don't get trigger-happy, Sheriff," Dallas said, raising his hands as he slowly turned to face the lawman. "I just shot a wanted outlaw in self-defense. You oughtta be considering writing out a pay voucher for me instead of acting like you're upset."

"We don't know what the hell you're talking about," a chunky man with a walrus mustache standing alongside Sinker Wilson growled, keeping twin pistols aimed at Dallas's chest. "But we do know what to do with murderers here in Devil's Gate."

Dallas glared at the rotund sheriff through slitted eyelids. "I showed you the wanted posters, Sheriff. My shooting Jasper Flatt did the state of Texas a favor. You should be thanking me."

"I would," Sinker Wilson said, his voice strangely cheery, "if you'd plugged Jasper instead of poor ole innocent Wilbur, who's laying over there deader than a doornail. All he's guilty of is looking like his twin brother."

This just keeps getting better and better, Dallas thought. "Whoever he was, that fellow drew on me. A man has a right to defend himself."

"Reckon he has a point there," the burly brown-haired man wearing a deputy's badge said. "I suppose we oughtta give him a fair trial before hangin' him."

"Yeah, I reckon," Sinker said with a shrug. "Bounty hunter, you can thank Deputy Garrick Sparks here for being so thoughtful. Now, using one hand, pull out that gun of yours nice and slow and drop it to the ground."

Dallas did as he was told. The way things were shaping up, any more talk would be wasted effort.

"I'll keep him covered," Sinker said to the deputy. "Go put the cuffs on him."

A moment later Dallas felt hard cold steel bite deeply into his wrists.

"Reckon he won't be killing any more honest citizens in Devil's Gate," Garrick said with satisfaction.

"I didn't know there were any," Dallas said.

The deputy stuck his guns back into their holsters, then came up with a knotted fist and drove it into Dallas's gut, dropping him to his knees.

"Listen up, bounty hunter," Garrick growled. "You give us any more guff, I'll take it right personal. And it ain't a good idea to rile the law here in Devil's Gate."

Dallas gasped. "I think the lesson's beginning to take."

"You can come on out now, darlin'," Sinker said, turning to look into the shadowy depths of the livery stable.

Velvet Dawn ran to the fat sheriff and embraced him.

"Thank heaven you showed up," she said. "That awful man was kidnapping me. He told me he'd kill me if I didn't go along with him."

"I'm glad to see you're beginning to appreciate the law," Sinker said. "Life's a lot less painful when a person fits into a community."

Dallas blinked his eyes into focus. He stood slowly and stared at the sable-haired girl standing in the shadow of the sheriff. Never before in his life had he felt so betrayed, yet he could understand Velvet Dawn's desire to stay alive. At least she appeared to have that option. He did not. "She's telling the truth about me making her come along."

"Git back to the hotel," Sinker said to Velvet. "This town needs pretty whores, they attract business." He added with a sneer, "Just remember, your line of work don't require a lot of walkin'."

Velvet Dawn spun and hobbled away without another word.

"Let's get our boy over to the jail, Garrick," Sinker said. "Then I'll go fetch the judge and begin rustling up a jury. With any decent luck we can get this trial over with before supper time."

Garrick Sparks nodded as he grabbed onto Dallas's arm. "It won't take 'em long for sure. Be nice to replace that Ruggles fellow. When the wind blows just so, he smells mighty gamy."

The sheriff said, "Can't go rushing things too much. Hangings are always a boon for business, and we both know how much Tiberius Poxon appreciates a prosperous town. Why, I'd bet folks will come from miles around for this event if we take time to get the word out."

"Don't rush any on my account," Dallas said.

"Today being a Wednesday"—Garrick's mustache cocked to one side as he thought—"I'd say a Sunday hangin' at three or four in the afternoon would be about right to get the most good out of him."

"I'll check with Poxon, but it sounds like solid thinking." Sinker turned to a tall gangly man with silver hair and a pockmarked face who had appeared from the shadows of the livery. "Howdy, Jack. Your showin' up saved me from runnin' around trying to find you."

The man called Jack eyed Dallas with cold eyes. "That's the bounty hunter?"

"Yep," Garrick said. "This feller here's the one who kilt poor Wilbur."

"You're Jack Flatt," Dallas said, not really needing an answer. The man he faced was simply an older version of the outlaws' pictures on the wanted posters.

"I am." The man's voice was like an icy wind. "And I also follow the teachings of the Good Book, sir."

Garrick smiled. "Jack always admires to quote that part about an 'eye for an eye' at all of his trials."

Sinker Wilson noticed the puzzlement cross the prisoner's face. "This is a small town, bounty hunter. We're forced to make do the best we can. Jack Flatt here is a business owner. He's also the mayor, an' when we need one—like now—he's the judge."

Chapter 10

This time the fortified gray stone jail looked a lot more imposing to Dallas Handley when Sinker Wilson prodded him inside with the hard steel barrels of his sawed-off shotgun. The rock walls were nearly two feet thick, with the metal bars in the small windows set in the center. A lot of military forts had been built of lighter material than the Devil's Gate jail. Breaking out of the imposing structure would take some of both time and luck. Considering the fact that the fat sheriff was planning to hang him three days from now, time was not on Dallas's side.

"You can't say I didn't treat you square, bounty hunter," the sheriff said. "Shucks, I let you keep your guns and gave you plenty of opportunity to simply ride off without even getting your hair mussed. But oh, no, you had to stick around an' shoot someone. I hope you can understand that I intend for you to draw a profitable crowd Sunday, to pay me back for all of those good intentions I went and wasted on you."

"Sheriff," Dallas said staring down the somber stone corridor lined with cells. "Jasper Flatt was a murderer and a wanted man. That story of him having a twin brother is a crock."

Sinker Wilson smiled thinly. "All you gotta do is convince the judge of that fact and you can ride away with my sincere apologies."

Dallas sighed. "Which cell is mine? I prefer one with a view."

Garrick Sparks poked him in the kidney with the barrel of his Colt. "Smart-mouthed son of a bitch. I ain't gonna give you a solid drop come Sunday. Dancin' around a lot while stranglin' slow always gives folks a better show."

"Garrick's also our hangman," the sheriff said. "Poxon pays him an extra sawbuck for the task."

"With everyone here so money-hungry," Dallas said, "it's a shame to let Jasper Flatt go to waste. He's worth two thousand dollars in gold, straight out of Austin, once his body's turned over."

The deputy stopped poking Dallas's kidney so hard. "Jasper's worth that much?"

"Put the bounty hunter in a cell," Sinker said with a sigh. "After he's tucked away, I reckon we oughtta gather up that body as evidence. Then we'll have ourselves a little discussion about how to cipher figures correctly when you're dealing with your boss."

Garrick Sparks jabbed with his gun. "Last cell on your right. I'm giving you one with a window for tellin' how much the bounty was. Don't expect no more favors come Sunday. My good nature don't extend to not putting on an entertainin' hanging."

"For some reason, I didn't expect it would." Dallas started down the dreary corridor. "I don't suppose I can send for a lawyer?"

"Of course you'll have one," Sinker said, his voice echoing off the stone walls. "We ain't never hung nobody without them having the services of Ike Clum. He might be a tad biased, him being the town undertaker who gets fifty dollars for a buryin', but ole Ike's got a way with legal words, that's a fact."

"Thanks for the window," Dallas mumbled as he walked inside the cell.

"I'll fetch your dinner from the Silver Baron. They're serving liver an' onions tonight," Sinker Wilson said after taking off the handcuffs and slamming the massive steel-barred door closed.

Dallas plopped down on the bed and stared forlornly out the tiny window. "Somehow I was coming to expect that."

"Y'all get some rest," Sinker said as he turned to leave. "Once we've held your trial, I'll come by and tell you how it turned out."

"I don't even get to be there to defend myself?" Dallas hollered at him.

"Like I said, bounty hunter. Ike'll take good care of looking after you."

"Ask the cook if I can have extra onions," Dallas shouted, but the chubby sheriff and his cold-eyed deputy had already gone.

From the dingy light seeping through the barred window Dallas decided it was coming evening. He rubbed sleep from his eyes and stretched to limber up from his nap. A closer look out the window showed that the thick smoke from Poxon's mining operations had been jammed by wind into the craggy gorge once again. A dull orange orb hanging low in the west told him it was earlier than he had first thought.

The rest was necessary to clear the dulling spiderwebs of fatigue from his mind. There was no doubt that he would be hung in three days. The town of Devil's Gate seemed to thrive on greed, treachery, and death. If he were to survive this manhunt, he would have to figure out some way to escape from the most formidable jail he had ever set eyes on.

Dallas took a dipper of water from a dented bucket, flicked out a dead fly, and took a tepid swallow. "Damn it!" He tossed the dipper back into the bucket. "Even the water here is evil enough to choke a goat."

He sat on the edge of the iron-framed bed, raised a boot, and laid it on his left leg. After a few minutes of fiddling with the heel, he had it turned open and the tiny Gem .22 pocket revolver he had stowed in the opening was in his hand. At a mere 3-7/8" in length, it was the smallest five-shot revolver built. He tucked the gun into his pocket, extracted the additional cartridges sewn into the leather lining, then returned the heel to normal.

From the other boot Dallas pulled out a small pocketknife along with a set of lock picks and a small coil of piano wire. It took him the better part of an hour to work the metal handle of the water dipper into two sections, each about four inches long. Once the piano wire had been securely fastened to the center of each piece, he had a quite serviceable garrote that could sever a man's throat in less time than it took to blink.

He heard the sounds of someone coming, and quickly stowed the garrote under his pillow.

Sinker Wilson stomped up to the cell door. "Ike Clum done a right smart job of lawyerin', bounty hunter. But you being guilty as John Wilkes Booth, there weren't no other outcome than the hanging we were all plannin' on."

Dallas snorted. "I'm glad I didn't disappoint the fine citizens of Devil's Gate."

"Nope, Ike'll get fifty dollars for putting you in the ground, Garrick another ten for the hangin', and I get two thirds of Flatt's reward money."

"While Tiberius Poxon's businesses will enjoy a flurry of folks coming in to delight in watching me hang."

"That's about the size of it, bounty hunter. To show my gratitude for your helpin' out the economy, I'm gonna let you have a visitor."

"Visitor?" Dallas shook his head in bafflement. There was not a single soul in this town he could fathom who would want to see him.

"Yep," Sinker said. "That whore you were trying to kidnap come to see you for some reason. Now don't you fret none. I done checked her over mighty close and she ain't hiding any gun or knife. I also made it plain to her that if she messes up our hangin', she would take your place."

Dallas felt that Velvet Dawn had quickly came up with that story of her being forced to leave with him to spare herself from Sinker Wilson's wrath, a darn good reason considering how sadistic the sheriff was. It puzzled him as to why she wanted to see him; since he was locked in jail, there was nothing he could do to help her.

"Send her in," Dallas said with a thin smile. "She's a pretty girl."

"Yep," Sinker Wilson said as he turned. "That li'l gal is a real moneymaker and an asset to the community. Reckon Poxon would have me drive needles under all of her toenails to keep her here." He chuckled. "Shucks, she don't make any money standing on her feet anyway."

Dallas forced himself not to pull out the small pistol and shoot Sinker Wilson. That pleasure he would have to put off until later. A distant rustling of skirts, then Velvet Dawn came limping down the dreary stone corridor. He was surprised to see the sheriff had let her come unescorted.

"I'm sorry about that kidnapping story," Velvet Dawn said in a low voice. "But both of us being in jail would keep me from trying to help you escape."

"This jail's the toughest one I've ever seen." He nodded to the tiny barred window. "I've every good intention of disappointing the good citizens of Devil's Gate come Sunday, but I'm sort of short on any good plan. Have you got any ideas?"

Velvet Dawn came close to the barred door, bathing Dallas in the delicious aroma of lilac perfume. "I thought about slipping you a gun through that window. Then I remembered Sinker always makes a prisoner back up to the bars and stick their hands through and handcuffs them before he'll unlock the door."

That's good to know. Dallas felt his spirits sink. "Do you have a plan that might work?"

"I was hoping *you* would. Being a tough bounty hunter, I figured on you knowing all about breaking out of jails and stuff like that."

"My job is generally putting them behind bars, not busting them out."

"Then I suppose it's up to me." Her lower lip began to quiver. "Dallas, I'm scared for the both of us."

"Buck up, girl. We're going to leave this damn hellhole of a town one way or another." Dallas forced a smile he didn't feel. "Tell me, darlin', can you send a telegram without causing yourself problems?"

"Vern Camper's the telegraph operator. He also works for Tiberius Poxon. Anything I send will be reported to the sheriff."

"Darlin', I've never set eyes on Poxon, but he is getting me riled. Do you have a pencil and paper?"

Velvet Dawn nodded and opened her reticule. "I

hope you're not going to just ask some decent lawman for help."

"Don't worry about that. I want you to send this message to Gus Boggles at the Concho Pearl Saloon in San Angelo." Dallas put the paper on the ledge beneath the window and began writing. After a while he handed her the message along with the pencil.

"I have no idea what this means," she said, studying the note with obvious puzzlement. "Is it some kind of code?"

"It is. The person who gets this telegram will be the only one that will know what it means."

Velvet Dawn took a long look at the garbled words: HELM IMPULSE JAG DEVASTATE GASTRIC HANDWORK IMPULSE THRASH DAUB SOMEWAY. Then she folded the paper and tucked it into her purse.

"You'll need money to send it," he said.

She nodded. "I had a few dollars hidden away. Sinker found them when he searched me before I could see you and stuffed all of it in his pocket as a 'fee.'"

"That man *is* a major annoyance." Dallas took a pair of gold eagles from his vest pocket and handed them to her. "I'm surprised he let me keep my money."

"I'm not. After you're hung Sinker can take all the time he wants to pick through your pockets."

"You go send that message straightaway, darlin'. San Angelo is some distance, but I'd venture before Sunday, Sinker Wilson, Tiberius Poxon, and a lot of folks here in Devil's Gate will have more to concern them than they've had to contend with before."

"I hope you're right, Dallas. The last person who talked about cleaning up this place came to grief."

"Who was that?"

"Bob Morgan, the day before he got shot full of holes."

Chapter II

"I thought I'd better get this telegram over here without tarry." Frank Deeter's sallow face was lined with concern as he handed the paper over to Barney Handley. "Looks like that boy of yours is fixing to get hung down in that new mining town of Devil's Gate."

Barney clucked his tongue and raised a stubble-bearded cheek. "And just how did you come to this brilliant conclusion?"

"It's a code any idiot could figure out. All anyone has to do is read up or down a set number of lines in the dictionary, for Pete's sake. And there ain't that many different dictionaries to make it much of a test; least-wise there ain't in Texas. And Gus Boggles plays the piano for you here in the saloon."

Barney Handley took a pair of spectacles from his pocket and squinted at the telegram. "I'd reckon there ain't no need for me to strain my peepers an' look for my dictionary. What's it say? All of it."

The telegraph operator took a moment to catch his breath. Since he weighed three hundred pounds, the short walk from his office near the train station to the Concho Pearl Saloon had winded him.

Frank held the message into the light of a dying sun that was shooting through batwing doors. "Dallas came straight to the point. At the twenty-five cents a word it costs, I reckon being economical is just good sense, but a tad more information would have been helpful."

"Just read the dang thing. I swan, if a body'd ask you what time it is, you'd tell 'em how to build a watch."

The telegraph operator snorted, causing a trickle of tobacco juice to ooze down a corner of his mouth. "It says: 'Help, in jail, Devil's Gate. Hang in three days. Son.'"

"See, Frank," the wiry, silver-haired saloon owner said. "That pretty much covered all the territory that needed covering and didn't wind you none."

"That's why I come running all the way over here. I thought it was something you would want to know about."

Barney Handley knew what the corpulent telegrapher was fishing for. He turned to the bartender and hollered, "Slim, give ole Frank here a draft beer and chips for four more. I'm appreciative of his help."

"Thank you, Barney," Frank said. "What are you planning to do about it?"

"I'm studying on the matter. Since his ma took pneumonia and passed away on me, that boy's all I've got in the world, so I reckon I've got no choice but to go down there and do what's necessary. Dallas might have gotten in over his head for a change."

"Being a bounty hunter's not known for being a safe occupation. That's why I learned a skilled trade. Morse Code is the way of the future. My services will be in demand for the rest of my days."

"Those days ain't gonna stretch out too far if you don't lose some of that lard."

"Being chubby's a sign of good health." Barney followed Frank as he headed for the bar and his waiting beer. The telegraph operator took a long drink, then asked seriously, "You going alone? I've heard stories about that town. It's an evil place. A preacher that got run out of there said, 'If God don't destroy that town, he owes Sodom and Gomorrah an apology.'"

"I've heard things about Devil's Gate myself. Supposedly, it's a mighty easy town to get killed in."

"Mining towns are all like that. You ain't answered me about going alone."

"Riding into that place with an armed posse might cause more harm than it'd accomplish. I reckon I'll grab a couple of my best guns along with plenty of ammo and head down there." He looked at the big oak Regulator clock behind the bar. "When does the next train going in that direction pull out?"

Frank spun the sweaty mug on the wood bar. "Eight o'clock this evening. It'll take you all the way to Fort Stockton. From there you'll need to ride a horse. Now Jonas Simpson has a livery stable down there. He's a cousin of mine on my Uncle Seth's side of the family; that'll be the ones who live up near Abilene—"

"I'll make certain to look him up," Barney Handley interrupted to keep his pudgy friend from rambling on. The saloon owner was a lot more concerned over his son than he showed. Three years ago they had worked out the code and agreed that it would only be used as a last resort. Dallas was resourceful; to have sent that message meant he was in trouble. Serious trouble.

"I wonder what Dallas is going to be hung for." Frank finished his beer, then tucked the chips into a pocket of his shirt. "Generally, he's the one who brings 'em in for that to happen to."

"I'll know when I get there." Barney took a long nine cigar from his pocket, bit the end off, and lit it.

"At least I've got three hours before I have to catch the train. That'll give me time to line up help that'll not rob me blind while I'm gone. Runnin' a saloon's a full-time occupation, I'm here to say."

"Well, thanks for the beer. I'll have 'em make out your ticket when I get back to the office."

Just as he reached the batwing doors, the bulky te-legrapher stopped and turned, his expression serious. "Watch your back trail, pardner. That's mighty danger-ous country you're heading for."

Barney Handley nodded his silver-cropped head, an artificial smile on his lips. "I'll fetch Dallas and both of us will be back home in San Angelo in a few days."

"I hope so," Frank Deeter said. He pushed open the batwings and was gone.

Chapter 12

Sheriff Sinker Wilson was in uncommonly high spirits when he brought in Dallas Handley's supper on Saturday. Even though Dante's Inferno Saloon was some distance away, the raucous noise of the crowd along with the cheerful, tinny sounds of a honky-tonk piano, echoed along the craggy gorge that cradled Devil's Gate, as if trapped there, like the acrid smoke from the mining operations.

"I brought you in a nice butter-fried steak tonight, bounty hunter." The corpulent lawman was almost drooling. "This time I went to the Worthington for your grub. Tiberius Poxon's wishing to show you his gratitude for drawing a profitable crowd. The Silver Baron leaves a little to be desired for good cuisine on occasion."

"I appreciate your concern." Dallas accepted the tray through a long horizontal slot built into the barred door to save the jailer from having to go inside the cell. "Most towns I've been in, the Silver Baron would be out of business the second day with the cook being hung instead of me."

"But you ain't in another town, bounty hunter, you're in *our* town." The fat sheriff moved aside to allow a tall, lanky man with dark hair, silver temples, and a decidedly pale countenance to step close to the bars. "Mr. Poxon here wanted to make your acquaintance and see what you looked like before the hanging. That event has a tendency to mess up folks' features."

Dallas set the metal tray down on his bed, then turned to study the mining mogul who ran the town with an iron hand. Velvet Dawn had been correct in that Tiberius Poxon was not what he had expected. The man's eyes were sparkling blue; he was not even dressed nattily, wearing Levi's and a plain shirt. The most remarkable trait Dallas noted was the cold, catlike manner and expression the man used to size him up.

"So you are the tough bounty hunter who came to Devil's Gate and shot the wrong man." Poxon's voice came across as almost musical in timbre. "I think you can see now that indiscretion of any type is frowned on here."

"From what I've learned about you," Dallas said, "it will only be a matter of time until you'll be standing where I am."

Tiberius Poxon tented his hands; his fingers were long and supple, nails clean and manicured. "But that seems to not be the case here today, *does it?*"

Dallas shrugged. "My supper's getting cold. If you just came to gloat, you've already got the job done."

Sinker Wilson growled, "Watch your manners, bounty hunter. You can hang with your eyes gouged out same as not."

"Tut-tut, Sheriff Wilson," Poxon said calmly, though stepping back a few feet from the cell door. "Mr. Handley is only reasonably upset. Considering the circumstances I want you to leave him be until the hanging. At that time, use whatever force is necessary, only have him at the gallows on time. I pride myself on punctuality."

Sinker Wilson snorted, "He'll be there all right. If he behaves himself, he won't even be bleedin' when Garrick puts the rope around his neck."

"Your efficiency will be rewarded, Sheriff." Tiberius Poxon gave a curt bow, turned, and was gone; his departing footsteps were so light they could not be heard against the hard stone floor.

"Pleasant fellow," Dallas said turning to his tray of food. "I'm surprised he hasn't gone into politics like the better class of crooks usually do."

"Poxon's going to move to Austin an' run for Congress," Sinker Wilson said before screwing down an eyebrow in thought.

Dallas removed the cloth from the tray, then the ornate pewter dome covering a large china plate. He blinked at the huge steak that appeared perfectly cooked, the heaps of sauteed mushrooms, mashed potatoes and gravy, corn on the cob, slices of buttered bread, along with a generous slice of peach cobbler sitting in a bowl of sweet cream. To add to his surprise, tendrils of steam showed the meal to still be piping hot.

"I suppose you could say this is a meal to die for," Dallas said as he salted and peppered the gravy.

"Poxon wants folks to eat at the hotel. That's why he pays Lulu Flatt to run the Silver Baron the way she does to convince folks of the right place to spend their money."

Dallas hesitated with the salt shaker. "Lulu Flatt. She wouldn't be any relation to Sam an' Jasper by chance."

"They were her darling boys, bounty hunter." Wilson chortled. "But don't fret none. I'll fetch your breakfast from the hotel if you promise not to act up none an' cause me problems at your hanging."

"I give you my word, Sheriff Wilson, that for another great meal, I'll cause you no more problems than Heracles did for Medusa."

Sinker Wilson's head lowered. After a moment he said, "See that you don't." Then he turned and stomped off, his departing footsteps echoing from the stone walls like dying heartbeats.

Chapter 13

An hour past the stroke of midnight. The bitter smoke from Poxon's mine boilers seemed to have been pushed down and concentrated by the darkness. Inside his cell, Dallas wiped soot from his eyes and watched tendrils of black smog waft through the tiny barred window, where they undulated eerily in the flickering yellow light of a coal-oil lantern to hang in the still air like bewildered spirits.

Dallas Handley was awake and alert as a cat on the hunt. He mulled his options over in his mind while listening to the distant din of music and laughter from the saloon. The fact that Velvet Dawn had informed him he would be handcuffed from behind severely limited how he could employ the small revolver in his pocket to advantage. He could always pull the gun and point it at Sinker Wilson in the hope that the fat slob would be smart enough to open the door to save his own skin, but considering the sheriff's behavior so far, he doubted the outcome.

It would be good to know if Velvet Dawn had sent the telegram. He had not seen or heard from her since the day of his arrest. There was, though he doubted it, a chance the girl had simply taken his money, bought a ticket on the stage, and was already long gone from Devil's Gate. Ladies in her profession *were* noted for such behavior. Making the mistake of trusting the wrong person in situations like the fix he was in could be fatal. He had best rely on his own resources.

Perhaps I might play sick, groan and moan, roll around on the bunk, then when Garrick or Sinker comes in to see what's wrong with me, I'll use my garrote. Then I can employ the revolver to make my escape. I should have thought of that earlier.

Dallas shrugged his shoulders in resignation. Those two idiots wouldn't come inside his cell if someone tossed a rattlesnake through the window and it had its fangs fastened onto his leg. It took a modicum of compassion to see why someone was writhing in pain. Sinker Wilson and the deputy would most likely simply enjoy the show from a safe distance.

The problem was, his options were becoming really limited, as was the time to do whatever needed doing. With the hanging set for noon, a mere eleven hours remained for even a bad decision to be made.

For the first time in all of his years of working as a bounty hunter, Dallas Handley began to understand the cold, harsh bone-chilling fear a prisoner felt before being executed. He decided that if he lived through this, he would consider showing a tad more kindness toward his prisoners in the future. At least the better-behaved ones.

Of course, he reminded himself, if his situation didn't show some rapid improvement, he wouldn't be dealing with any more outlaws in the future.

Dallas spun to look up at the window. A fluttering noise caused him to think that either a big moth or possibly a small bat was trying to fly through the narrow bars. It was neither. A small stick could be seen tapping away between a couple of the steel ribs.

He stood and placed his face close to the opening. "All right, who's out there?"

"Well, don't go shouting to the whole dang-blasted world that you're fixin' to get busted out," a wonderfully familiar voice scolded from the murky darkness.

"Dad," Dallas said, lowering his tone, "am I glad to have you show up."

"Reckon you are at that, sonny boy. We stopped by the saloon to sorta wash out the trail dust. There's a real passel of folks looking forward to your hangin'."

Dallas asked, "Who's *we?*"

"It looks like you'd finally got yourself in a real fix," Frank Dutton's gravelly voice had never sounded more welcome. "Besides, the railroad's looking for whoever stole a stack of tickets, so I'm gettin' paid to come here anyway."

"Glad to know you aren't being put out none," Dallas said through the bars. "Either of you two come up with a good idea about how to bust me out of here?"

"Now that *was* a dilemma," Barney said. "But Frank here had heard about this jail bein' built like a fort, so we brought along lots of extra dynamite."

"Dynamite!" Dallas nearly shouted. "I don't care if you blow up the damn jail, but I'd rather not be inside it when you do the job."

"Quit your bellyaching." Frank's voice again. "Dallas, you've always had a tendency to complain too much. We're betting you've got a nice thick mattress on your bunk."

"Yeah, I do," Dallas acknowledged.

His father said, "Then, sonny boy, I'd highly recommend that you cover yourself up with the thing. After you do lay down as far from this wall as you can get."

"Dad," Dallas hissed, "you can blow a hole further up the jail. I've got my lock picks. I can open the door and—"

"We don't have time to hold a town meeting," the railroad detective's gravelly voice said. "I'd advise you to get doing what your pappy advises."

"This ain't a discussable issue," Barney said sharply. "Frank an' me are heading for a safe place. This here fuse seems to be burnin' faster than it oughtta be."

"Oh, shit," Frank's voice yelled, followed by a scurry of rapidly departing feet.

Dallas had barely gotten the thick mattress stripped from the bed when there was a flash of light. Then the thick stone wall of the Devil's Gate jail came toward him like a wave on the ocean, followed by the blackness of unconsciousness.

Chapter 14

Dallas Handley thought he could hear the angels singing. He decided it would be best to keep his eyes closed and study on the matter. By all accounts dead people did not feel any pain. That ruled out him being dead. His head throbbed worse than with any hangover he could remember. Carefully he flexed first his fingers, then toes. They all seemed to be where they should be and functioning.

At least those idiots didn't blow me completely up.

He took a chance and moved his right arm. *So far so good.* After testing the other arm and both legs, it was time to open his eyes and check out his surroundings. If he wasn't still in the Devil's Gate jail, he decided he might not shoot either Frank or his dad for a few days out of gratitude.

"Well, looky who finally finished his nap," Barney Handley said cheerfully. "Welcome back to the land of the living, sonny boy."

"You nearly killed me trying to save my life," Dallas said. He sat up and still heard the angels singing. That was when he realized the ringing in his ears from the explosion might take a while to go away.

"It's afternoon and you ain't dangling from a gallows like some Christmas tree ornament," Frank said coming inside what appeared to be a rude line shack. "I'd expect a tad more gratitude to be in order."

Barney lit a long nine. "You listen to your friend. Dynamite's tricky stuff to deal with and costly to buy. It was my idea to place those extra fifty or so sticks we brung along up near the front of the jail to cause a distraction for the jailer when he came running out to see what the ruckus was."

"An *extra* fifty sticks!" Dallas shouted, causing a sharp pain to stab at his left eye. "How much powder did you idiots use, for the love of Pete?"

"We found it was more economical to buy a full case," Frank said contritely. "That gave us at least a hundred sticks to work with."

"Sure did catch that jailer off guard," Barney said. "After we blew that hole in your cell, he come scamperin' out the front door just when that other charge went off."

Frank clucked his tongue. "Reckon they'll be picking pieces of him out of cactus for days. I told your pa we should have put that bomb further away, but he insisted we set it right where that big wood door would open straight onto it. I just hope the fellow that got blowed up wasn't an honest lawman. I'd feel plumb bad about it if that was the case."

"You can rest your conscience, Frank," Dallas said. "Aside of the little gal who sent that telegram, the whole damn town getting blown up would be a considerable improvement."

"Didn't figure you cared much for the place," Barney commented, blowing a smoke ring. "We heard tell you killed Jasper Flatt's twin brother by mistake. That a true happening?"

Dallas shook his head, causing a fresh stabbing pain over his left eye. "That story was a crock. Sheriff Sinker Wilson likely wanted the reward money. In Devil's Gate, Judas Iscariot would be outclassed in the asshole department by most anyone you run across, with Tiberius Poxon heading the list."

"Heard about him," Frank Dutton said after spitting a wad of tobacco juice at a horned toad that had wandered inside looking for a bug. "Owns all the mines and most of the town. Folks say it's wise not to cross him."

"My boy generally don't pay close attention to what folks say," Barney commented. "Reckon this might be a lesson for him that'll take."

Dallas winced when he stood. More than a few of the flying rocks from the jail wall had managed to bruise even through the thick mattress. It was, however, better to have been knocked around some than hanged. He forced a thin smile at his father and railroad detective friend. "Thanks for breaking me out."

Frank Dutton nodded in acknowledgment. "I'd reckon you're welcome. If'n your pa hadn't stopped by for a visit when he got off the train in Fort Stockton, I wouldn't have been here until next week. Now, I'm party to blowing up a jail along with a lawman. Behavior like that can look bad for a man in my position, or it would if the Texas Rangers weren't coming to check out the place. I got a telegram saying Captain Luke Gardner was heading for Devil's Gate to straighten out the town. Said he's starting with the sheriff and going on from there. One of the benefits of working for the government is not having to be economical with words when you send a wire."

"I'd like to have waited for the Rangers," Barney said, "but they're coming all the way from Austin, might not make it here for some time. With you being sorta pressed for time, we decided to come on ahead."

"I appreciate that." Dallas reached out and took a long nine cigar from his father's shirt pocket. "Just where are we anyway?"

"About five mile north of Devil's Gate is all. Frank and me ran across this old cabin on our way into town. Seemed like a good place to hole up and let you finish napping."

Dallas lit his cigar. "The fellow y'all managed to blow up was a deputy by the name of Garrick Sparks. He was also the hangman, so I'm not going to pine away for him. The worst of the lot there is named Tiberius Poxon. He has a manager by the name of Harry Latts, who I've not set eyes on. . . ."

"Harry *Latts!*" Frank Dutton exclaimed. "Hell's bells, I've gotten flyers on him. He isn't wanted in this country, but in Canada. For all accounts the man's a hired murderer and damn good at his job."

"That explains him being in Devil's Gate," Dallas said. "The place is a natural draw for folks like him."

"Tell us about the sheriff, Sinker Wilson," Barney said with concern. "We have some considerable interest about him maybe putting together a posse. Having a deputy along with a big chunk of his jail blown up would be a powerful peeve to most sheriffs."

"Sinker is a fat tub of lard who does what Poxon tells him. The man's a sadist who drove needles under a cute gal's toenails to make her testify she got raped so they could hang a fella. Poxon wanted the man's interest in a silver claim, and chose that method to get it." Dallas walked over to a window with the glass broken out and stared across the bleak desert. "But to answer your question about a posse, I'd say that's a distinct possibility, considering the clouds of dust heading our way from the south."

Frank and Barney ran to look over his shoulder.

"I brought you a Colt .45 Peacemaker and a Winchester '73," Barney said. "Has your head cleared up enough for you to shoot straight?"

"Yeah, Dad, I'm coming around." He went to the rifle his father had nodded toward, picked it up, and levered a cartridge into the chamber. The caliber was 44-40, a slug of lead big enough to stop any man. "If Sinker Wilson's leading them, I want to be the one to repay him for that gal. Her name's Velvet Dawn and I owe her my life for sending you that telegram."

Barney nodded. "When you run low on ammo let us know an' then we'll start shootin' at 'em too."

Frank Dutton took out a small leather-covered brass telescope from a saddlebag. "Let's take a gander at what we're up against." He clicked it into focus and studied the approaching dust cloud.

"Well, what do you see?" Barney asked impatiently.

"I'm trying to figure it out myself. Dang'dest thing I ever seen in all my born days."

"You oughtta consider that we might have considerable interest in what's heading our way," Dallas commented.

Frank Dutton clucked his tongue. "It's the biggest dang wagon you've set eyes on, and to top off the matter, the thing's being pulled by a pair of elephants."

"Dang it, Frank," Barney snapped. "Dallas was the one that got his head whacked. What excuse do you have for pickin' a time like this to go crazy?"

"I can see it without the spyglass," Dallas said. "Frank's right about the elephants. The things a circus wagon heading out of Devil's Gate."

The railroad detective said, "Reckon we can put the

guns away, from the looks of things. There's nothing I notice coming our way but that one big wagon."

"I've always had a hankerin' to see an elephant," Barney said, lowering the hammer on his Henry rifle. "They ain't a common sight in West Texas."

"Let's go visit when it comes past," Dallas said. "Whoever's driving the thing might tell us some information about what's going on in town."

"Dang, look at that thing move!" Frank exclaimed. "I always thought elephants to be slow. Looks like I was mistaken."

"Sure ain't no horses could keep up that pace for long and live," Barney said.

A few moments later the three men stepped out of the rude cabin to wave down the rumbling wagon. A skinny black man wearing a turban shouted some strange words at the elephants and lightly touched the one he was riding on the forehead with a long stick. The huge coach groaned to a stop.

"Greetings, gentlemen." A door swung open to allow a smiling bald man dressed in a garish red suit to jump out. "How may I be of service? My name is Omar Lassiter, owner of Lassiter's traveling circus, with trained elephants and, of course, my lovely wife, Princess Noria, who performs the Oriental art of belly dancing, among other feats."

Barney stared at the huge elephants, obviously transfixed.

"Go and touch them, my good man," Omar said with a bow. "They are quite gentle, I assure you. Halim, my driver, has given them an order to stop. They will not move until he motions for them to do so."

"You're coming from Devil's Gate," Dallas said, anxious to get to the point. "What's going on there?"

Omar flashed an angry look over his shoulder. "That

town is the worst place we have ever been in. I thought with the hanging drawing a crowd, business would be good. Alas, the trip was a washout, I fear."

"I'm proud of you, sonny boy." Barney kept his gaze fixed on the elephants. "Few people draw a circus for their hanging."

The circus owner cocked his head at Dallas. "Are you the one they blew up the jail to break out?"

"Could be."

"The sheriff's tolerable pissed off about all the damage. He said he can always hire another deputy, but stonework costs considerable."

"I can see you've made the acquaintance of Sinker Wilson. He's as unfeeling as a rattlesnake."

Omar shook his head. "I think I prefer the snake after what that man went and done. . . ."

The door to the huge circus wagon opened to allow a slender young lady to exit. She was dressed enticingly and the only girl Dallas had ever seen to go around with a bare midriff. The event turned Barney's attention from the elephants. "Dear," the raven-haired beauty said, "are these men going to rob us?"

"No, darling," Omar said. "I have a feeling they're not. I notice the man in the suit is wearing a badge. I think we're fine."

Dallas said, "I'm a bounty hunter. Frank Dutton, the fellow with the badge, is a railroad detective. The old codger needing a shave is my dad, Barney Handley. My name is Dallas."

Omar wrapped an arm around his shapely wife's bare middle. "Noria here and I heard all about you, the bounty hunter who shot the twin brother of the man you was after. I'd reckon a mistake like that's an easy one to make."

Dallas shook his head. "That story's not true. I shot

a wanted murderer by the name of Jasper Flatt after he drew on me."

"We just came in to try and drum up some business. None of that's our affair," Omar said with a shrug.

Noria spoke up. "The sheriff was in a dither and acting greedy. He wanted us to pay fifty dollars for a permit, so we left right after the hanging, no reason to stay in a place like that if we can't make some money."

"Going to Fort Stockton, then maybe on to San Angelo or possibly El Paso," Omar said. "There's gotta be better folks most any direction from Devil's Gate."

Dallas blinked in bafflement. "You said there was a hanging?"

"Yes," Noria said, dabbing at a tear. "It was awful. I hope to never witness anything that terrible again."

"The little gal died hard," Omar said. "A pretty little thing, had a crippled foot to boot."

Dallas felt building fires of rage and guilt in his soul. He took a moment to compose himself well enough to speak. "Her name, did you hear her name?"

Omar nodded. "Yep, the sheriff said they were hanging her because she helped break you out of jail and kill that deputy. They called her Velvet Dawn."

Chapter 15

Frank Dutton had seen the fires of killing hate flare in people's eyes before, like they had just done in Dallas Handley's. The beautiful young "Princess" Noria had not. She gave a slight gasp, spun, and jumped back inside the massive circus wagon.

"I take it that poor gal they hung was a friend," Omar said softly. "Our sincere condolences."

The railroad detective nodded. "She sent Dallas' daddy the telegram that brought us here to bust him out of jail. I'm of the mind there will be hell to pay now. The Texas Rangers are on their way to Devil's Gate an' clean up the place, but I've known Dallas too long to expect him to wait around."

Dallas turned his head toward the circus owner and stepped close. His movements were stiff and measured. He noticed trepidation in the bald-headed man's eyes when he extended his hand. "I want to thank you for telling me about what happened. Velvet Dawn suffered having needles driven under her toenails by Sheriff Wilson. Then that tub of lard went and hung her for no reason other than to put on a show. I intend to settle things with that man straightaway."

Barney yanked his gaze from the huge elephants that were patiently staring at the bleak horizon. "Ain't no sheriff worth his salt does stuff like my boy says he did. I'd expect him to be permanently out of office mighty shortly."

"Tiberius Poxon is who's responsible." Dallas shook Omar's hand. "I'll settle with him right after I've put Sinker Wilson in the ground." His cold expression melted slightly as he glanced into the open door of the wagon. "Ma'am, you and your husband have a safe trip." Then he spun and headed into the shack.

Omar Lassiter looked at the two remaining men. "If the Texas Rangers are on their way, you should try to talk him out of being rash. There were a lot of tough-looking men in that town. I'd expect the sheriff to pin stars on a lot of them."

"Reckon he will at that," Barney said biting the end off a long nine cigar. "I'd venture we've got plenty of ammo to handle 'em."

"I often think Noria and I should have stayed in the East." Omar motioned to the driver as he climbed on board the garish wagon. "The Texans seem to be especially prone to violence." He gave a wave as the elephants began the wheels turning once again. "But I do wish you fellows the best of luck."

Barney nodded and watched the wagon slowly creak away. After a moment he said to Frank, "Reckon I can finally say that I've seen the elephant."

"Let's hope you get a chance to brag about that back in San Angelo. I'm of the opinion we're getting ourselves fixed for a season of some serious killing."

"Looks like it," Barney said as he began heading for the open cabin door. "But I intend to do my best effort to make sure the only people who get shot are deserving of it."

"Yeah," Frank said hurrying to catch up with the older man. "That would be my intentions too."

Dallas was thumbing shells into the cylinder of his Colt revolver. He slammed it closed, spun the cylinder one last time, then slipped the .45 into the holster that he now wore low on his hip, the end tied with a leather string to his leg gunfighter-style. Turning to his approaching partners he said, "You fellows ought to check your loads too. I advise a cartridge under the pin. There's likely going to be a need for all of the firepower we can muster."

Frank Dutton thought for a moment about trying to calm Dallas down and waiting for the Texas Rangers. Then he asked, "This gal they hung, how old was she?"

"Velvet Dawn's real name was Constance MacDougal. She had jet black hair and would have been twenty her next birthday."

The railroad detective envisioned a pretty girl of about his daughter's age being lynched in front of a jeering crowd.

"Let's ride," Dutton said.

"Now don't go gettin' dithered up." Barney placed a hand on his son's shoulder. They were crouched in the shadows of a copse of juniper trees high on the side of a craggy, boulder-strewn ledge overlooking Devil's Gate. "Frank's just checking out what we're up against to keep us from riding into a hornet's nest an' get ourselves kilt like a bunch of greenhorns."

"Yeah," Dallas acknowledged. "That's the smart thing to do." Even from the considerable distance he could see the body of Velvet Dawn dangling from the gallows. A fiery lump grew in his throat when he noticed she was wearing that same red-print dress she had on the first time he had seen her in his hotel room. He doubted his ability to speak without choking up, so he decided it best to keep as silent as he could, knowing his companions would understand.

Frank Dutton took the telescope from his eye. "I've never been in a town that would leave anyone hang from a gallows. That's plumb disgusting."

"You're learning Sinker Wilson," Dallas mumbled.

Barney squinted when he looked at the town. "It don't appear too much is going on, at least from what I can make out through all of this damn smoke."

"Makes the place seem dirty as it actually is," Frank said offering the spyglass to Dallas. "Reckon that fits."

Dallas pulled his gaze from the distant gallows. "The smoke and fumes gets a lot heavier at times. It's sort of like God is trying to hide this evil place from his view."

"And making a tolerable success of it," Barney commented, rubbing his red eyes.

Frank shook his head. "From what I can make out, the town's quiet. Looks like the sheriff's got some Mexicans working on putting his jail back together. Other than that, I can't see anything exciting going on. They sure don't seem to be any posse being put together, which I find strange."

Dallas folded the telescope closed and handed it back to Frank. He would see more of Devil's Gate than he cared to shortly. "I figured on Sinker Wilson to lay low. He's a coward at heart and he's got Jasper Flatt's body that's worth two thousand dollars to attend to. The man's motivated only by greed. That's a trait that causes him to stay around, because Tiberius Poxon's a wealthy man. Besides, there's no money in chasing me down. It would also be a considerable risk to his health."

"You saying that sheriff's too dumb to think three

men might just ride into town and plain shoot him full of holes," Barney said.

Dallas grabbed another long nine cigar from his father's pocket, bit off the end, and lit it. "No, he's mean but not stupid. Those cannons in the walls of that jail of his are loaded with chains. You can also bet he's pinned a few stars on some of the worst thugs and ruffians he could hire to protect his worthless hide."

"Damn," Barney spouted. "I've seen what chains fired from a cannon can do back in the war. They go spinning wild all over the place, cutting not only the riders but also the horses into bloody shreds. They're to be avoided no matter what."

"Boys, I've been giving this matter some serious thought," Dallas said, his voice tinged with anticipation. "Right here's a comfortable place to wait till dark. What do you say we play ourselves a hand of cards and get some rest. I've got an idea that'll take care of a lot of our problems."

"How about blackjack?" Frank said.

"Dad's too good at cheating at that game," Dallas said. "How about five-card stud or hearts? He's only moderately skilled at cheating in those games."

Frank Dutton extracted a deck of cards from a pocket in the vest of his pinstripe suit. He deftly began shuffling. "Five-card stud it is. Then after I've cleaned y'all out, I'll expect Dallas to explain his plan and how we might live through it."

Chapter 16

A new day was being born bloody on the craggy horizon east of Devil's Gate. It was an auspicious beginning. Even the oppressive acrid smoke from Tiberius Poxon's mining operations had been scoured from the steep canyon by a gentle breeze from the south, giving the air a strange feeling of sultry cleanliness.

Sheriff Sinker Wilson noticed none of this, however, as he trudged to his job after spending the night with a decidedly second-rate whore in the Worthington Hotel. He briefly regretted having hung the only really pretty girl in town, but business is business. After all, he hadn't had to pay the whore. That benefit was only one of many that came with being the sheriff in a town run by a man like Tiberius Poxon.

Sinker hesitated for a few moments to survey the damage to his jail those stupid outlaws had done when they had freed the bounty hunter. It galled him to have to deal with Mexican stonemasons. They were lazy and moved slower than molasses poured in January.

"Damn pepper-bellies will take until a week after the Second Coming to patch my jail up," the sheriff muttered as he continued on. "It's just good that they work cheap."

He noted with satisfaction the distant body of Velvet Dawn swaying from his gallows. A few harsh lessons like that were what it took to keep a town in line. Even though he doubted anyone would be foolish enough to challenge his iron rule, he had gone along with Poxon's advice and sworn in a half dozen of the best (or worst) men in Devil's Gate to act as deputies. To his way of thinking, it was an unnecessary expense that came out of his share of the protection money the business owners not in league with Poxon had to pay or face expensive, often fatal, consequences. However, thinking on the matter, having a few more guns to back him up was not a bad idea. There certainly were a lot of people wishing him harm these days.

Sinker Wilson frowned when he came to the remains of the once thick door to his massive jail. If that idiot Deputy Garrick hadn't run outside at the exact moment he did, the door would still be intact. He shook his head at the odds, then opened the smaller temporary door to go in and relieve Jonas Baragree, his new night deputy.

"What the hell!" The fat sheriff drew his Colt and tried to make sense out of what he saw. His nice big shiny oak desk was overturned with chairs stacked on top of it; a long table was on the opposite side of the room, also overturned. Sinker Wilson stared at the long, narrow corridor leading back into the dark line of jail cells.

"Jonas," he barked. "Get your lazy ass out here and tell me what's going on."

Only the silence of stones answered his entreaty. For the first time in a long while, the ponderous sheriff felt shivers of fear licking at his spine. "I ain't in a mood to play games here, Jonas."

More silence. He batted his eyes to focus in the dusky interior. That was when he noticed the glowing red spot of a burning cigar waving in the depths of the stone corridor.

"Jonas." His voice wavered. "If that's you, get out here or I'll . . ."

Sinker Wilson's heart skipped a beat when, in the shadows, he recognized one of his cannons in the hallway. And it was pointed straight at him.

"Oh, God!" Sinker exclaimed when he made out Dallas Handley standing alongside the cannon. "Don't!"

"Velvet Dawn sends you her regards," the bounty hunter said, his voice cold as a snake's hiss.

The last thing Sinker Wilson ever managed to do on this earth was fire a single desperate shot at Dallas Handley, who dropped quick as a prairie dog behind the cannon. The last thing the fat sheriff ever saw was the red-hot end of a cigar touching the firing vent of the cannon. After a flash of bright light he was plunged into the bitter darkness of eternity.

"Dad was sure right about a chain," Dallas commented. "I'm not certain how it managed to whack Sinker Wilson into three pieces, but I am gratified with the results."

Dallas admired the aesthetic manner in which the spray of crimson being blown out the jail door from the fat sheriff's dismembered body blended with the red glow of morning. Then he pulled the wads of cotton from his ears and turned to the ashen-faced Deputy Baragree.

"Now let that be a lesson," the bounty hunter said to Jonas, who was locked in a cell, shaking like an aspen leaf. "Sinker Wilson's dead and you are not. If you stay in here nice and quiet, no matter what you hear going on, I might consider simply letting you ride out of town after all of this is over." He grinned evilly. "What's your feelings about that happening?"

Jonas Baragree's mouth was so dry from fear he could only muster a hoarse stutter. "I—I'll be glad to stay here an' be quiet as a mouse."

"Smart man." Dallas stuck the cigar into his mouth, took a contented puff, and blew a smoke ring at Deputy Baragree before sauntering outside to meet up with his father and Detective Dutton.

The trio met at the foot of the stairs leading up to the gallows where Velvet Dawn's small body swayed in the building breeze.

Barney Handley stared with narrow eyes at the corpse. "That was one pretty girl."

"There is no way this Poxon character can get by with such a cold-blooded act as hanging a woman," Frank growled. "The poor girl never even got a fair trial. I expect Captain Gardner will most likely put Tiberius Poxon in her place and do it within minutes after setting hands on that man. Luke ain't one to abide goings-on like this."

Dallas dabbed at an eye that had gotten something in it. Then he climbed the thirteen steps, took out his sheath knife, wrapped Velvet Dawn's cold body with his free arm, and cut the rope.

"Hey, what the hell you think you're doin'," a burly man dressed in dirty overalls with a glistening tin star pinned over his heart yelled. "That body's supposed to stay there until—"

The man's tirade was cut short when Dallas's bowie knife slammed into the deputy's chest only an inch below the badge. He gave a startled wheeze, then dropped onto the dry dirt to begin shivering like a clubbed fish.

Barney went to the man and checked him for weapons. Often a mortally wounded person could still manage to draw a gun and shoot someone. The man grew limp while Barney was patting his pockets.

"He wasn't armed," Barney said.

"That won't do," Frank said taking a small rusty pistol from his boot. He tossed the revolver onto the dirt beside the still body. "Now, as far as the law's concerned, he was armed and drawing on you."

Dallas nodded agreement, then cradled Velvet Dawn's body in his arms and carried her down from the gallows. "I'm going to place her under the platform where she'll be in the shade. There's some killing that needs done before I can make proper arrangements."

Frank Dutton grabbed the bone handle on the bowie knife and jerked it free. He wiped the blood from the blade on the man's overalls, then handed the knife over to Dallas when the bounty hunter came from under the gallows.

"Obliged," Dallas said to Frank as he sheathed the bowie. "I trust that pistol's not valuable."

"Nope, I paid only fifty cents for it because the hammer spring is busted and the cylinder's rusted shut." He shrugged. "It's not a wise move to leave a bad man with a gun that'll shoot, even if he appears to be dead at the time."

"Thanks for retrieving my knife." The bounty hunter turned and glared down the main street of Devil's Gate. A few people had heard the cannon fire and stepped outside to see what was going on. They gave the three men a quick look before darting back into the confines of their buildings.

"I can't help but wonder just how many men that

Sinker Wilson fellow went and pinned a badge on," Barney said, checking the loads in his ten-gauge double-barreled shotgun. "That'd be helpful information to let me know how much ammo to pack."

"Don't matter," his son said jacking the lever on his Winchester rifle. "I plan to start shooting anyone with a gun and not stop till they're dead as a doornail."

Frank Dutton came to join them. He carried Barney's Henry rifle, which he had won from him in last night's poker game. "Let's go clean up this town."

Chapter 17

"Well, Mr. Latts," Tiberius Poxon said to the slender man with long black hair who had his eye to a large brass telescope that was mounted on a tripod in the upstairs window of Poxon's mansion overlooking Devil's Gate. "Tell me what's going on down there. That cannon was only to be fired by Sheriff Wilson during an emergency situation."

"From studying the mangled pieces of a body laying in front of the jail, I believe the remains are those of Sinker Wilson. To make matters even worse, I see three men carrying long arms walking toward town. Surprisingly, one of them is wearing a badge."

Tiberius Poxon took a dainty sip of black tea from a china cup. "I was warned the Texas Rangers might possibly be coming here, but I didn't expect them to do more than make a report to Austin. I have considerable influence there to squelch any report." He set down the teacup. "Let me have access to the telescope, Mr. Latts."

"Yes, sir," Harry Latts said stepping to one side. At twenty-eight years of age, the slender gunman prided himself on having killed one man for each year he had lived. Whoever the three men were down there who had obviously blown away the stupid Sheriff Wilson, they would be no match for his wonderful skills with a gun. No match at all.

"The man in the middle is that bounty hunter, Dallas Handley," Tiberius said. "He was the man Sheriff Wilson let break out of my jail, which forced me to hang that girl. I don't know who the other two are, but any man with a badge is troubling. I think it best that they are all killed right away. It will also be an added lesson to the citizens of Devil's Gate that I am not to be trifled with."

"A little patience, Mr. Poxon. I gave explicit instructions to the late sheriff to hire more deputies, placing at least two on each side of the main street. Those three men down there should be walking into a deadly volley of cross fire that will cut them to shreds."

"Very good. I can only hope Sinker Wilson hired the right kind of help."

"If they fail, *I* won't."

"And that, Harry, is why you are paid so well."

The gunman returned to the telescope. After a brief moment, his brow became lined with puzzlement. "What the hell?"

"Boys, let's hold up here a minute," Dallas Handley said. "I think we're overlooking a safer way to do this job."

Barney stopped in his tracks and gave his son a skewed expression. "Well, spit it out, sonny boy. I ain't made it to the ripe old age I'm enjoying by not listening to good advice, especially when it concerns avoiding getting shot at."

Frank nodded. "I'm going to join your pa on that. There's undoubtedly going to be at least a couple of misguided souls in this town who are tolerably upset about having their sheriff blown to smithereens."

"Boys," Dallas said motioning with the barrel of his Winchester to the sprawling, white three-story mansion perched on a hill that overlooked the town like a priest from an altar. "You know how best to kill a snake." He did not wait for an answer. "You cut off its head. Tiberius Poxon is the head of this stinkhole. Once he's gone the place might improve enough to become civilized."

The railroad detective wore an evil smirk as he studied the towering, palacelike structure that must have cost the unbelievable sum of thirty thousand dollars. "Dallas, my friend, it's times like these that always makes working with you so downright enjoyable. This is going to be *fun*."

Barney Handley nodded his understanding, then turned to study the jail. "I reckon since I was an artillery officer back in the war, it's up to me to figure out how to hit the joint. Let's go drag a couple of those cannons out. Then we'll check out the armory an' see just what all we're got to shoot with. Then we'll proceed to blow that big-ass fancy house Tiberius Poxon's so dang proud of clean off that mountain."

"These are six-pounders," Barney said, affectionately patting the black cylinder of the one cannon pointed straight down the main street of Devil's Gate. "These things can tear up a patch, I'm here to tell you. We'll keep this one that's loaded with chain to discourage anyone who decides to take offense with our actions."

"If'n they saw what happened to Sinker Wilson, I'd expect they won't bother y'all none," Jonas Baragree said, keeping his eyes averted from the bloody pieces of his former boss.

"Thanks for the help, Deputy," Frank Dutton said. "These cannons are dang heavy to move about even if they are on wheels."

Barney said, "Just the barrel of the thing weighs over eight hundred pounds, to the best of my recollection."

"I hope your memory can come up with how to load and fire one of these things," Frank grumbled. "I'm not in favor of trying to figure out shooting a cannon by trial and error."

"Your luck, the same luck that won you my trusty Henry rifle that you're holding, my detective friend, is in good hands. I've fired this same type of artillery over a thousand times."

"Then let's get with it, Dad," Dallas cautioned. "It's not wise to give folks a lot of time to think things through, especially the bad folks."

"Deputy," Barney said, turning to the second cannon, "grab that tail piece and scoot it over about six inches to your left." A moment later he growled. "Now move it about a foot to your *other* left."

"Which of these shells are we gonna lob first?" Frank reached into a wood chest and held up an obviously heavy black ball.

"That one will do fine," Barney said. "But take care not to set off the scratch fuse. Those things have about a three, maybe five-second delay before blowin' up. It's preferable to have that event happen over where we shoot it."

The detective paled, then gingerly returned the shell to the box. "I'll wait until you tell me what needs done."

Barney held out a device strange to everyone but him. "It's a gunner's quadrant," he remarked. "This is what we use to compute the angle of fire. That big house ain't much over a quarter mile away, but it's higher than we are. I've got to factor that in."

"You do what's necessary," Frank Dutton affirmed. "Ain't nobody here in a dither."

"Looks like the gunpowder's already in bags," Dallas said, holding up a dirty sack he had taken from another of the boxes they had dragged from the armory.

"While you've got that powder in your hands, sonny boy, bring it over here an' dump the entire pound an' a quarter of it down the barrel. Then bring me that long rod with a rag on one end—we call that thing a sponge rammer. The solid end is used to tamp in the shell. Before the next shot, the sponge is dipped in a bucket of water and the barrel is swabbed out to make certain there ain't no hot spots to set off the new charge of powder all by itself. Always exciting when that happens."

"I'll fetch a bucket of water," Jonas Baragree said, already running toward the jail.

Barney clucked his tongue. "Fidgety fellow there. Now back in my day we were being shot at during all of these procedures, a circumstance that understandably can cause anxiety, but back then—"

"Dad, aim the darn cannon," Dallas grumbled.

"Youg'uns today ain't got no patience." The old artilleryman carefully took his measurements and made the final adjustments. "We used to use a device called a 'linstock' for the fun part, but not having one, a cigar will work just as good."

"I know." Dallas bit the end off a fresh long nine and fired it with a match.

"This town is becoming a peeve," Frank Dutton commented as he pointed a finger down the distant main street. "If I see the situation correctly, there's a couple of the stupidest yahoos in Texas charging us with just pistols."

Dallas looked to where Frank was pointing and sighed. "They're from Arkansas, most likely. Texans, even the dullest ones I've ever met, wouldn't charge a cannon with nothing but a pistol."

"They're in range, sonny boy," Barney said with resignation.

Dallas shrugged, turned, and stuck his freshly lit cigar into the firing port of the first cannon.

"Hell's fire an' tarnation," Jonas shouted as he came from the jail carrying a bucket. "That shot not only blew both of those fools halfway down the block, but went through a horse and then through the side of the livery stable. I ain't never seen nothin' like that before in all my born days."

Barney squinted through the cloud of powder smoke. "Yep, I'd say those two idiots won't be troubling us any in the future."

"While the lesson's being digested by those who didn't care to join in charging us, maybe we oughtta lob a shell at Poxon's shack." Frank reached down and grabbed up the same cannonball he had held earlier. "I'm anxious to see just what one of these things can do."

"I heard another cannon fire, Mr. Latts." Tiberius Poxon refilled his china cup with tea from a silver carafe, taking time to carefully measure in a level teaspoon of sugar before continuing. "Kindly tell me what you see going on down there."

Harry Latts kept an eye glued to the brass telescope. "Tell me, Mr. Poxon, have you made plans for a hasty exit should a situation arise that would give you reason to do so?"

Poxon snorted and reached for his tea. "I have, but

for the life of me I cannot envision that happening. Why do you ask?"

Harry Latts said nothing. He clicked the powerful telescope into clearer focus in time to see the bounty hunter touch a smoking cigar to the firing vent of a cannon. A cannon that was pointed straight at him.

"Mr. Poxon," Latts said, jerking away from the spyglass. "I believe the answer to your question is headed our way."

Chapter 18

Barney Handley squinted as he watched the cannonball he had sent flying toward Tiberius Poxon's mansion explode on the front porch, blowing out windows, doors, and sending pieces of lumber taking flight in all directions. The old artilleryman's stubble-bearded face mirrored his satisfaction.

"Dang!" Frank commented, awestruck. "A few feet higher and that shell would've gone inside the drawing room. I reckon you really do know how to shoot that thing."

"You boys quit lollygagging," Barney said. "Swab out the barrel an' reload it while I crank up the elevation a mite. All gunpowder varies in strength from one batch to another. Now that I've got a feel for the stuff, we can start doing some serious damage up there."

Dallas did not hesitate. He ran the wet sponge down the cylinder, loaded a fresh charge, then rammed home another ball. "Dad," he said with a nod to the other cannon. "I'm of the mind we ought to reload that other one too. I doubt any more of Poxon's men are dumb enough to charge us, considering what happened to the other two, but we are dealing with idiots here."

Frank Dutton gave a sinister snort. "You could sure say those last two fools don't have the guts to do that again." His expression turned serious. "But I agree we oughtta load it. After all, we *are* in Devil's Gate."

"There isn't any more chain," Dallas said. "I suppose a shell would do to get their attention."

"Load 'er up, sonny boy," Barney said, walking over to the open chest of ammunition. He sorted through the contents a moment before straightening, holding a shell. "This here one's loaded with grapeshot. I'll set the elevation so it'll explode on the ground about in the middle of Main Street. Bein' in Hell is preferable than standing around close when one of these things go off."

Dallas rammed home the fresh charge of powder. "Considering the town, I wonder if they'd notice much difference."

"Better company, most likely," Barney said, cranking the muzzle lower. "Son, I want you to grab up a big handful of tow outta that box an' ram it tight again the ball. It'd be embarrassing to have it roll out the end once I get the thing pointed low enough."

A moment later the cannon had been loaded, aimed, and the firing vent primed with a fresh charge of gunpowder from a powder horn.

Frank Dutton turned to study Tiberius Poxon's mansion. He frowned when he noticed fingers of flame tipped with black smoke shooting from a blown-out window. "Dang it all, it appears that shot must have dumped over a coal-oil lamp or two. I was really looking forward to shooting at the place some more."

Dallas took a healthy puff on his cigar, then handed the cigar to his friend. "Go ahead. I'd hate to give those folks up there the mistaken feeling they could simply go put that fire out at their leisure."

The railroad detective beamed like a kid entering a candy store when he touched off the charge. The cannon spit a tongue of fire from its barrel, followed by a cloud of smoke and an ear-splitting roar. Scant seconds later, the entire left portion of the lower floor of the huge mansion exploded outward on orange tentacles.

"Wow!" Frank Dutton stared gleefully at the burning mansion. "Can we shoot another round?"

"They can't do this to me!" Tiberius Poxon screamed at a blown-out window. "I'll have them all hung."

"Sir," Harry Latts said with urgency in his voice. "I believe they've already done it. Your house is on fire and I really don't believe those men are through firing that cannon. I suggest you gather your most valuable assets and do so without delay."

Poxon's dark blue eyes sparked with pinpoints of hate. "Yes, Mr. Latts, you are correct in your observations, but I *will* kill every man down there who had any part in this debacle."

"Of course you will, sir." Harry Latts winced when a burning beam crashed through the ceiling of an adjoining room. "For now, however, I advise a quick exit."

Tiberius Poxon gave a harrumph, then strode to an ornately engraved safe that sat against a smoking wall. He bent over the combination to keep prying eyes from watching him spin it. When he realized the folly of that action he simply moved the dial to the correct position and opened the heavy iron door.

"I have your saddlebags, sir." Harry Latts held them out to his employer, who began stuffing them with cash and colorful stock certificates.

"The gold coins are too heavy to carry many of,

Harry. Stuff your pockets with all you can. Consider it a bonus for your help and loyalty."

"Thank you, sir. I shall, however, merely keep them safe for you. I pride myself on exhibiting fealty to those who engage my services."

Tiberius grunted and kept filling the saddlebags. A former riverboat gambler on the lower Mississippi, Poxon understood all too well the foibles of men's souls. A preacher would steal the coins from a dead man's eyes if he thought God had his back turned to him for a moment. A liberal application of force, often deadly force, was the only thing that ever kept people in line. And he fully intended to keep Harry Latts in line. Then, when he was no longer a necessity, dispose of the detestable gunslinger posthaste.

Poxon noted with relief that his most valued assets— deeds, reports, and stock certificates for the valuable silver mines—fit into the relative safety of the saddlebags. There was likely a solid five thousand dollars in bulky gold coins that weighed well over three hundred pounds still in the safe. He had no choice but to abandon the gold to be destroyed along with his beloved mansion. *Dallas Handley is a dead man. I will kill him slow for what he has done to me.*

An ominous groan from above prompted Harry Latts to pull the jammed saddlebags away. "We must go, sir," he said, his voice tinged with fear. "The ceiling could collapse any second."

The mining mogul snorted as he stood. It galled the very essence of his being to leave money behind and run, yet he knew he must. A distant boom from one of those damned cannons that fat slob of a sheriff had bought for some reason gave an added urgency to the situation.

"Let us not tarry, Mr. Latts."

When Tiberius Poxon turned to leave, Harry was already out the door. Scant seconds later, just as Poxon bolted from the once-splendid mansion where he had envisioned entertaining congressmen and senators, another explosion caused the house to collapse into a smoking, burning heap of rubble.

Somehow, Harry had managed to have two saddled horses at the ready. Poxon tossed the saddlebags over his favorite horse, a sturdy roan, hoisted himself into the saddle, and spurred the startled mount into a run. His instincts were proven correct when another cannonball landed to completely demolish his private livery stable.

"Damn that man," Poxon yelled over his shoulder.

"I shall be glad to oblige you on that, sir," Harry Latts answered loudly over the clopping of steel-shod hooves on hard desert varnished rocks. "But I do believe we should regroup and choose another time for it to happen."

"Yes, Mr. Latts," Poxon said, his voice venomous. "But not too long from now, not too long at all, I will extract my just revenge."

"Dang." Frank Dutton had his telescope out. "There's a couple of scallywags riding away. Let's see if we can hit 'em with a cannonball."

Dallas grabbed the spyglass and focused on the distant departing dust cloud. "That one man's Tiberius Poxon and unless I miss my guess, the other yahoo is none other than Harry Latts. If we can lob a shell on top of them, I'm all for it, save chasing after 'em later."

Barney shook his head sadly. "Be a waste of ammo. A moving target ain't easy to hit, an' besides that, they're nearly out of range."

"Shucks." The railroad detective was obviously disappointed. "We just got it reloaded."

Barry cranked up the leverage, then kicked the tail-piece over a few inches. He nodded to Frank. "Touch 'er off."

Through the cloud of smoke the men watched a juniper tree explode several hundred feet behind the fleeing horsemen.

"Well," Dallas sighed, "at least they know we saw them heading west."

"And that a lot of folks are really pissed off at 'em," Barney commented. "Hangin' a little lady's something they can't run from. Tiberius Poxon will have a price on his head once Captain Gardner and the Texas Rangers show up."

Dallas Handley turned to face the town. "Boys, let's go have a visit to see if anyone in Devil's Gate's still loyal to that bastard. Once we get that settled, I have a matter to attend to, then I'll be off. Tiberius Poxon and Harry Latts are on the run, and I've been chasing outlaws for a lot of years."

"Yep, sonny boy," Barney said, his bearded face turned up in a grin. "Now we've got ourselves a manhunt."

Chapter 19

"I must say." Frank Dutton grabbed a sweaty mug of beer from the bar of Dante's Inferno Saloon and took a healthy swallow. "There doesn't appear to be any love lost in this town for Poxon. I've yet to meet a single person who's not happy to have him gone."

Harry Dinkman, the ponderous bartender, gave a grin. "Y'all can say that again. I built this saloon with my own two hands only to have that son of a gun claim it was on one of his mining claims. The choice he gave me was either sign it over and work for him or get hung for trespassing. I'm of the mind that the Rangers will see to it I get my property back. That's why you boys are drinking for free."

The telegraph operator, Vern Camper, said, "Most everyone here in Devil's Gate has been kowtowing to Tiberius Poxon for far too long."

A number of blank stares caused Vern to add, "The word kowtow means to bow down to, act in a fawning manner."

"Yep," an unkept miner said. "I'd reckon that pretty much covers it, but I'd hate to be an educated man an' have to look up words in a dictionary just to know what I was sayin'."

Barney Handley was enjoying his fifth beer along with his fame as the artilleryman who had destroyed Poxon's imposing mansion. "If that sheriff hadn't been a cheapskate an' bought a better-quality gunpowder, I'd have lobbed that first cannonball square through his front door. Too bad because that's what I'd call a door knocker that won't be ignored."

The bartender dumped a dead fly out of a mug and refilled it. "The bonus came when that shot down Main Street chopped apart not only the last two gunmen Poxon had still working for him, but then luckily went through that horse and rubbed out Jack Flatt, who was blacksmithin' inside the livery stable."

"Too bad about the horse, though, she was a good one," another miner commented. "But ain't nobody'll miss any of the Flatts. That's simply good riddance."

"Reckon Lulu will break camp now that all of her family's gone," Harry Dinkman said. "I might oughtta buy the restaurant from her. If somebody actually started serving decent food, that place would do a good business."

Dallas Handley stood alone at the front of the bar, silently staring out the batwing doors to the distant gallows while idly spinning his untouched first mug of beer. He had yet to lose his feeling of trepidation about this town. Even thought most of the citizens of Devil's Gate had welcomed them as conquering heroes, the tiny cold pinpricks of warning still played at the nape of his neck. *Perhaps it's just that I've yet to settle with Tiberius Poxon for hanging Velvet Dawn.*

"You . . . you sent word that you wanted to see me," a scarecrow-thin, obviously nervous old man wearing a pair of gold-framed spectacles low on his hooked nose stammered, shaking Dallas from his reverie.

"I take it you're Ike Clum?"

"Uh . . . uh, yes, sir, I am. And I sincerely wish to apologize for not being able to convince Judge Flatt not to hang you." The man was forced to take a deep breath before continuing. "But I assure you I'll give back the money I was paid to bury you, once there's someone to return it to."

"You can settle down." Dallas slid his mug of beer in front of the distressed fellow. "Have a beer. I don't care about what happened before. That money was Poxon's so go ahead and spend it. In short order he'll have no need for it. I called you here to talk about the girl they hung in my place, Velvet Dawn."

"That was a terrible thing they did. I tried my best to convince Sheriff Wilson and Mr. Poxon to simply cancel the hanging, but I was told that wouldn't be good for business and to shut up because I had already been paid to bury someone. . . ." Ike jolted as if he had been shot. "I . . . I'll bury her. It's just that the sheriff told me in no uncertain terms to wait until the birds had picked all the meat off first."

Dallas cocked his head and stared off into the distance, looking past the quaking undertaker. "The dead deserve to be treated with respect, even here in Devil's Gate."

"Yes sir, Mr. Handley, sir, I fully agree."

"Her body is under the gallows. I want you to fetch her and put her in a coffin, your best one, then fix her up as well as you can."

"I am a good undertaker, and pride myself at my job, but I . . . I . . . must remind you how much a coffin and embalming costs."

Dallas took a leather bag from his vest and tossed a

hundred dollars in gold coins to ring on the wooden bar. "That will cover it?"

Ike Clum's eyes widened. He grabbed up the money without hesitation. "I have a top-grade mahogany box, and my wife Nelda can get her a nice burying dress. We'll give her a first-rate send-off, I promise."

"I don't want you to put her in the ground." Dallas never took his eyes from the horizon. "I promised that little lady I'd take her from this place one way or the other. I'm just sorry it'll have to be in the back of a wagon, but I intend to honor my word."

"Of course, Mr. Handley, I'll give her my best embalming and keep her in a cool place until you're ready to leave."

"It may be a spell. Sinker Wilson I've already settled with, but I intend to chase down Tiberius Poxon, then show that man all the care and compassion he showed Velvet Dawn."

"Yes, sir, I understand. I must say that I have been burdened with four of the most torn-up bodies I have seen since the war. Sheriff Wilson was the worst—I have yet to find all of him—and Jack Flatt's head was cut completely off. Since you were the man responsible for all of this work and expense on my part, I don't imagine you could . . ." Ike Clum realized with a start that he had possibly gone too far. "I'll take good care of the lady, Mr. Handley. I give you my word on the matter."

Dallas Handley glared at the undertaker as he grabbed the mug of beer in front of the wide-eyed man and took a long drink. "And I give you *my* word that if you don't honor your promise, I'll settle your hash without batting an eye when I get back to this town."

The undertaker spun. "I'll get right on it," he said over his shoulder as he ran from the saloon.

"I must say, sonny boy," Barney said with a wry grin,

"that you've got a way with handling folks, yep, yep. But it is good to see you're mellowing out. Not too long ago that fellow would've needed to see a sawbones to get all the holes corked that he'd be bleedin' from."

Dallas shrugged. "It's been a tiring day."

Frank Dutton had overheard the conversation, and made his way through the crowded saloon to stand with his two friends. "For the most part, I'd venture the folks of Devil's Gate miss Poxon about like a carbuncle."

"People of his ilk are no different than a cancer," Dallas said, still staring out the batwing doors to where twilight was beginning to claim the day. "A doctor uses a knife to cut a cancer out of a patient to save a life. I use a gun to accomplish the same task. It's just sometimes hard to know when to stop cutting."

Frank nodded. "I'll keep an eye on the place until the Rangers show up. I telegraphed the railroad and filled them in on what all's happened. My bosses want me to assist Captain Gardner as a favor. That undertaker *will* do what you paid him for."

"Thanks, Frank," Dallas said turning to his friend. "I appreciate everything you've done except that part about nearly blowing me up with too much dynamite."

The detective shrugged. "Don't be so picky. I thought we done good, considering that was the first time either one of us ever used any dynamite."

Barney clucked his tongue. "Dallas has always had a tendency to complain, pay him no mind." He finished his beer, set the mug on the bar, and gave a look outside at the gathering shadows. "I reckon we'll both be heading off after Poxon an' Latts at first light."

The bounty hunter cocked an eyebrow. "*We?* I figured you'd be heading back to San Angelo to run that saloon of yours."

"No problems there. I've hired me a bartender by the name of Billy Boggs. He's honest an' trustworthy."

"You're sure about that, Dad?"

"Heck, yes. I shot him in the foot the last time I caught him skinnin' me out of a quarter. He knows my aim will improve if he has any further failings of honesty."

Dallas said, "It'll be nice having you along. Mostly manhunts are rather lonesome affairs. Reckon an extra gun along with a card game by the campfire will make this one a more agreeable experience."

"Don't forget to bring back enough of Poxon to identify," Frank reminded them. "I'm betting Captain Gardner will have a bounty waiting for you when you get back."

Dallas's brow creased with thought. "Now that you've brought up the matter, there's a two-thousand-dollar dead outlaw by the name of Jasper Flatt laying around this town someplace."

"I'll ferret him out," Frank said. "Give me something to do while I'm waiting."

"There'll be a three-way split of the reward," Dallas said. "I suppose it's the least I can do after all that money you spent on dynamite."

"Appreciate it." Frank smiled upon his freshly refilled mug of beer. "You boys have a successful trip."

Dallas placed a hand on his father's shoulder. "We'll be back just as soon as we've settled with those two."

"How many do you see down there, Mr. Latts?" Tiberius Poxon asked in a quiet voice. The two men were hunkered beneath a finger of rock, looking down on a lone way station used by the Overland stage.

Harry Latts squinted into the red haze of a dying day. "It appears to be just a single-family operation. I count only one man, his wife, along with a couple of girls maybe ten to twelve years old."

"I am certain we are being pursued. Fresh horses are imperative for us to make our getaway to where I can hire men to help me regain my town."

"Fresh horses and water will also be necessary for any pursuers."

"Quite correct, Mr. Latts. I feel a tinge of regret for being forced to kill not only the people down there, but also every horse, save the two we choose to continue on with."

"That is only a reasonable move, sir." Latts checked the loads in his Colt. "It'll be dark shortly. I suggest we simply ride in, give those folks a friendly wave, then when we're too close to miss, kill them where they stand."

Tiberius Poxon gave a thin grin. "Perhaps they will have some supper cooked. I'm quite famished."

Harry Latts holstered his pistol. "I'm sure there will be. After we have dined, I also suggest we burn the station house. Any pursuers will also need food. If we leave absolutely nothing for them, it will be to our advantage."

Tiberius Poxon tilted his head to listen to the song of a distant pack of coyotes that were welcoming the coming night. "You may expect a generous bonus when all of this is over, Mr. Latts, a *very* generous bonus indeed."

Chapter 20

When Dallas and Barney Handley came riding around a bend on the mountainous stage road, they both noticed the circling of black turkey buzzards against a crystal-blue sky before they caught the pungent smell of burnt wood and flesh.

The country going west from Devil's Gate was, as Barney aptly proclaimed, "So dratted worthless it wasn't worth stealing from the Indians." Treeless, cactus-studded, jagged mountains jutted upward from waterless plains as far as the eye could see. Only an occasional windmill, squeaking an entreaty for grease in the ever-present wind, pumping a few gallons of foul-tasting water each day, made any crossing of this wasteland possible.

The Overland Stage Company maintained way stations at quite a few of these life-giving windmills. Horses tired easily after many miles of pulling a heavy stagecoach through hot desert and over rugged mountain roads, so numbers of horses were maintained at these places. Fresh animals were hooked to the stage by the attendant while the passengers remained on board. This allowed for fairly rapid transit across the bleak wastelands. What Dallas and his father were to discover at this particular way station, however, would shock and anger the duo beyond anything they had heretofore experienced.

"This has to be work of the Apache," Barney spit, reining his horse to a dusty stop. "But I never heard tell of any Indian that'd kill a horse."

"No Indian is savage enough to do what happened here. This is the work of two white men, Tiberius Poxon and Harry Latts." Dallas gave a sigh, dismounted, and tied his horse to a creosote bush. He walked over and studied the nude, ravaged body of a once-pretty blond girl, possibly twelve years old.

"The bastards raped her," Dallas spit. "From the looks of it, she was strangled after they were done. Poor little thing." Without another word he went over to his horse, took a felt blanket from his bedroll, and covered the pitifully small body.

Barney's green eyes were mere slits as he stared past the bloating corpses of dead horses to survey the black, smoldering remains of the way station and the smoking stagecoach that was in front of it. "Looks like the little gal's the only one they didn't burn or at least try to. Gonna be an unpleasant task sorting what's left of these bodies."

Dallas took a bandana from his pocket and held it to his nose in hopes it might help diminish the stench of burnt human flesh. It didn't. He poked his head briefly into the window of the stagecoach that, for some reason, had not completely burned as had the way station.

"Counting the jehu and shotgun guard," Dallas said after a gagging cough, "I see four more bodies inside, looks like maybe two are women, but there's no way to tell for sure. My guess is the stage pulled up and nobody thought anything was amiss until they got cut down by bullets. Then, I'm guessing, they tossed in a gallon or two of coal oil and lit it."

Dallas strode past the horses pulling the stagecoach that were dead in their harness. He noted silently that each had been shot behind the ear. He grabbed up a double-barreled shotgun from the dusty earth and opened the breech. "This was most likely the guard's. The poor bastard was caught so unawares he never even got a chance to fire a shot."

Barney had dismounted and tied his horse. He felt as if he was back in some mournful, bleak battlefield of a long-ago war. The six dead horses still tethered to the stage brought the number of slaughtered animals to twenty-two. After another day of lying beneath a blazing West Texas sun, their bellies would burst from bloat and the stench would become unbearable. Both the animals and humans needed to be quickly buried after being dusted with quicklime to keep coyotes from digging up the corpses. But not only did the two men not have even a shovel, the outlaws who did this abomination were getting farther away with each passing moment. It both galled and saddened Barney to leave the dead to be eaten by buzzards.

Dallas glared at the horizon that shimmered in the heat of a dying desert day like a mirage. "You know why those bastards did this."

"Yep, son, I do. They know they're being trailed. And whoever's after 'em will need water, fresh horses, and food. From the looks of things, all we can do is push ahead with tired mounts an' only what water we've got in our canteens."

"I'm betting the stage simply pulled up at the wrong moment. Maybe a few minutes later, the guard could've settled with 'em, instead of being caught unawares."

Barney shook his head sadly at the three charred

bodies he could make out lying in the still-smoking ashes of the way station. "Reckon none of that matters now. Son, I never got to set eyes on either Tiberius Poxon or that Harry Latts, but I swear on the memory of these poor folks that I'll not rest until we've killed the both of 'em."

"That's a promise to be kept, Dad. Let's take a check on that rock tank the windmill used to feed before they burned it. Maybe we'll get a smidgen of the luck we'll need to keep on this manhunt."

The duo stood side by side staring at the corpses of two dead dogs floating in tepid, coal-oil-polluted water inside the tank beside the remains of a burned wooden windmill that stood stark against the desert like the blackened skeleton of some huge beast.

"These people are the worst I've crossed paths with." Dallas's voice was a low menacing growl. "I'm not stopping pursuing those bastards if I have to walk."

"Me neither, son, but they *are* doing what it takes to slow us down long enough for them to make a getaway."

Dallas turned to look down the empty road. A lone dust devil winding its way across the desert floor was the only thing moving in the stifling heat. "There will be another stage through here. When it comes, maybe we can get some water off them."

"Yep, but if they turn back to Fort Stockton to fetch the law, it won't do us any good, considering the direction we're fixin' to head."

"I feel awful about leaving that little girl unburied." Dallas tilted his hat to keep the lowering sun from his eyes. "We ought to take time to at least cover her with some rocks, keep the scavengers from her until the law can take the body to a town and give her a decent burial."

"I'll pitch in, son. It's the least we can do to show a tad of respect for the poor thing."

A half hour later, the two Handleys stood and stretched after placing the last heavy stone over the makeshift grave of the small corpse. Fiery red fingers shooting through patches of clouds on the western horizon told them night was approaching.

"Be easier on the horses traveling at night," Barney said, lighting his next-to-last cigar. "Cooler anyway."

"Slow and deliberate is the pace. There will be another way station a few hours ride from here. I only fear we'll encounter more carnage there. Tiberius Poxon and Latts are far more evil and determined than I'd ever figured them—or anyone—to be."

"That situation presents its own problem."

"I know, Dad. There's not a single shred of evidence nor anyone left alive to testify as to who committed this massacre. If those bastards manage to make a getaway from us, they can simply claim they weren't even in the area when any of this happened and most likely manage to have a lawyer get them off scot-free."

Dallas put an iron set to his jaw. "I don't intend for that to happen."

"I don't either, son. Let's go after those murdering sons of bitches."

"You hearing that stagecoach coming was quite fortuitous, Mr. Latts," Tiberius Poxon said, spurring his horse into a faster gait. "Not a single person there expected us to begin shooting them."

"That was bloody work, but there was no other choice, sir. With good luck we will lose any pursuers before El Paso."

"I was especially gratified with your idea of making it look like an Indian raid. If the harebrained lawmen who investigate the happening go after the Apache, so much the better. I have always looked upon those red savages with the greatest of loathing. Their raids on my shipments of supplies have been costly, quite costly indeed. I would relish seeing their complete eradication from the face of God's good earth."

Harry Latts lit a long, black Mexican cigarillo. "I felt bad about having to abuse the girl, but it was necessary to make it look like an Indian attack. Often, in my line of work, I am forced to do distasteful things to accomplish my tasks."

"I understand completely, Mr. Latts. Do not let the matter concern you any farther." Tiberius Poxon tilted his head back and sniffed the air. "Why, I do believe I smell the aroma of chili cooking. Perhaps the next way station is just beyond the next bend."

"It will be coming up soon, sir. They are generally only several miles apart."

"Then, Mr. Latts, I believe another 'Indian' raid to be in order."

"Sir, I'm looking forward to the task."

The two men rode out onto a flat mesa of rock to look down upon the lonely way station that sat beside a creaking wooden windmill. Both felt their jaws drop in utter amazement.

"What the hell?" Tiberius Poxon finally managed to gasp.

Chapter 21

Beside the open water tank, a skinny black man wearing only a white turban and skimpy, billowy loincloth was washing down an elephant using a long-handled brush. Another pachyderm stood patiently alongside, playing its long snout in the rock tank, occasionally flipping water onto its huge gray back. A gigantic garish red circus wagon was parked in front of the way station. There also appeared to be as many as a dozen children of various ages scampering about, laughing mischievously.

"I suggest, Mr. Poxon," Harry Latts said, "that we retreat into the shadows and observe this situation. I do not feel any hasty moves on our part to be in order at this time."

Tiberius nodded and joined his companion in urging their horses back beneath some jutting overhead fingers of red rock. "That's the same traveling circus I had Sinker Wilson run out of my town. I have always thought base entertainment of such lurid sort to be sinful and disgusting in the extreme."

Harry Latts cocked his head at that statement, but he had worked for men of Tiberius Poxon's ilk for far too long to risk a comment. He made more money in a week being a hired gun for rich men than his father had ever made in an entire year of sweating his life away trying to scratch out a meager living on forty acres of Missouri black land dirt. Harry was not only good at his job, he had found that even more than the money, he enjoyed the killing.

"I believe, sir," Harry Latts said, eyeing the way station from the relative obscurity of shadows, "there were only two men in that circus wagon, and one rather attractive woman, who tended to sordid dress." It was generally a good idea to pander to an employer, especially when they tended to be a lunatic like Tiberius Poxon.

"You are without doubt accurate in that observation. Disposing of those disgusting circus people will be an improvement for all of Texas." Poxon lowered his brow. "The children won't present us any problems. Let's wait here and count the men who might actually present a challenge when we ride in."

Harry Latts nodded his agreement. "Patience *is* a virtue."

The western horizon flared in brilliant crimson, then waxed and waned. It was as if Heaven was a ship that had caught on fire, burnt nearly up, and was now slowly sinking into a drab sea of blackness.

Dallas Handley and his father rode side by side along the dusty stage road, carefully pacing their thirsty horses. The horrors they had left behind weighed like an anchor on the men's souls.

"When I was a boy growing up in Lawrence, Kansas," Barney said, a plaintive expression on his bearded face, "my folks used to haul me to church every Sunday come rain or shine. I remember the white-haired old preacher would pound his fist on the pulpit and swear that every man had a soul that was worth saving.

"Well, son, I was coming of the mind he might be right. Then on August twenty-first back in '63, a date I've got branded in my memory, William Quantrill an' his band of cutthroats came riding into town looking for a feller by the name of James Lane. They wanted to burn him at the stake for some reason I've forgot. Well, Lane skedaddled an' Quantrill got in such a dither, he ordered over four hundred and fifty men an' boys to be shot an' killed to teach folks a lesson that he weren't to be trifled with.

"For some reason of fate, me an' my family all got spared. But I saw that old preacher, his hands tied behind his back, made to kneel an' a bullet shot into his head. Right up until that shot was fired, the parson was praying for the soul of the man who was gonna kill him. I often wonder why God went an' let that happen. Now I find myself feelin' the same way about those poor folks at that way station."

Dallas took a long nine cigar from his vest, bit off the end, and started to light it. Then he hesitated, extracted the last one from his pocket, and hauled it over to his father.

"Thanks, sonny boy."

"We're going to need to stock up on cigars next chance we get. Being out of smokes is another grief to deal with." Dallas studied the dying sun for a moment. "That old preacher might have been right about everybody having a soul, but I've dealt with some that were so black and evil, I wonder if Satan will have 'em or why. Seems to me if God was being reasonable, he'd consider their souls to be not worth anything and simply rub them out for all eternity."

"I reckon us being mere mortals, we'll never know what goes on in the Big Feller's mind."

"Ineffable is the only way to describe it, Dad."

Barney lit the smoke, turned to his son, and clucked his tongue. "This is what I get for lettin' you go all the way to high school. A simple everyday nickel word would do just fine, but oh, no, you have to go an' come up with one that's worth a whole six bits."

"That word is big enough to choke a Philadelphia lawyer, I reckon. Ineffable means something that can't be expressed or uttered."

"Nope, I can utter it just fine. It's the understandin' part that's the difficulty."

Dallas slumped slightly. He was growing weary of chasing after outlaws, bringing them in to be hung, only to have them replaced in short order by a seemingly even worse crop of thugs. "You know, Dad, it's times like these that cause me to wonder if there really is a God, or if he really is up there in Heaven watching all of the evil that gets done down here, why he doesn't get off that gold throne of his and lend a hand."

"Oh, there's a God all right, sonny boy. I just don't think he gets to Texas very often."

Dallas sighed and studied a yellow orb that had begun rising in the darkening sky. "Looks like an Apache moon tonight. The Indians won't attack at night unless it's light enough for their souls to find the Happy Hunting Ground if they get killed."

Barney gave a slight chuckle. "Hard to believe, ain't it, the bloodthirsty Apache Indians being afraid of the dark."

"They have their beliefs, we have ours. I sometimes wonder if either of us are right."

"Don't go gettin' all melancholy on me, sonny boy. Times like these call for focus. It's after a person lives through 'em that there's time for being a philosopher."

Dallas said, "Sometimes a good ideal can give a person that focus you mentioned. An English philosopher by the name of George Henry Lewes once wrote, 'The only cure for grief is action.'"

"Wish that feller was here now. We could use another gun." Barney savored a long drag on what he knew would most likely be his last cigar for a long while. "But there's a thought I can agree with. I only hope we can catch up with those bastards right soon and settle their hash. We're about out of smokes."

Dallas gave a silent nod. The duo had talked themselves out. Beneath a twinkling canopy of stars that cradled a killing Apache moon, they continued their slow, deliberate pace westward.

Harry Latts was in a pensive mood. He sat cross-legged atop a flat shelf of sandstone overlooking the way station, a fist held thoughtfully to his left cheek. Tiberius Poxon stood a few feet behind him, hidden in the deep shadows of an overhanging shelf of rock.

"We are fast losing the daylight," Poxon observed.

"There's a full moon tonight. That will give us all of the light we require."

"I can see no reason to tarry. There appear to be only three men. The two women and all of those screaming urchins down there will present us no difficulties."

"A little more patience, sir. There are people still milling about. When they all set down for supper will be the time for our attack."

"*Excellent* deduction, Mr. Latts. Your percipiency is commendable. Most commendable."

Harry Latts took his fist from his cheek. The gunman

never ceased to be amazed as to how, when people became moneyed, especially crazy people, they tended to use fancy words. He had only gone to school for two years, his services being required on the family farm. Latts felt fairly certain, however, that he had been paid a compliment. "Thank you, sir, I . . ."

Tiberius Poxon quickly noted the reason his employee's words had trailed off. From out of the last fires of a western sunset came a creaking prison wagon with steel barred windows. Ahead of the wagon rode two armed cavalry men, behind it at least a dozen more.

"I do believe an obstacle to our attack has arrived," Latts said.

"Perhaps they will simply change the horses and proceed," Poxon said hopefully.

"Not a prison wagon guarded as heavily as this one. That many guards are never assigned to a transport unless there's a good reason. I'm betting there's a real hard case in that wagon. That's why they'll hole up here for the night. Ambushes are a lot harder to pull off in the daylight."

Tiberius Poxon said, "I have chosen keeping to the stage road to avoid giving lawmen access to the telegraph lines along the railroad line to the north. Yet I fear the passing of a full night might give time for word of what happened to the way station to make it here."

Brilliant deduction, you stupid idiot. Harry Latts slithered back beneath the rock ledge and stood alongside Poxon. He took a moment to measure his words carefully. "That is a very likely occurrence, Mr. Poxon. I believe we should return posthaste to our horses and proceed west."

Tiberius Poxon growled, "We need fresh horses. Ours have been pushed to the point of exhaustion.

Also, we have no water left in our canteens and I'm famished."

There is a fortune in his saddlebags, Harry Latts thought. Only the reputation for loyalty he had so diligently worked to build kept him from quickly and quietly cutting Poxon's throat and riding away.

Latts said, "It would appear that the playing field has become somewhat more level. Now *we* are the ones who must push on under adversity instead of our pursuers."

"How do we know anyone is after us?" Tiberius whined. "Surely that prison wagon will be off in the morning. Then we can attack the way station after getting a good night's sleep."

"Any bounty hunter, Texas Ranger, or competent sheriff can follow tracks. There has been no rain to obscure ours. Every hoofprint we have left since leaving Devil's Gate is still there, plain as a railroad track to someone who knows how to read sign."

Even in the deep shadows of a gathering night, Harry Latts noted with some pleasure that Poxon's face paled considerably.

Tiberius Poxon swallowed hard. "I agree. Let's get on those horses and ride away from here."

Chapter 22

An Apache killing moon was hanging high in a bejeweled, satin-black sky when Dallas Handley and his father finished telling the wide-eyed group of men gathered around a long table in the way station about the massacre that had occurred at the next stage stop to the east.

Cavalry Major Layton Green's dark eyes sparked like flint when he said from across the table, "If what you say is true, how am I to believe you two men had no hand in those terrible killings?"

Before Dallas or Barney could answer, a lanky master sergeant by the name of Cole Burke spoke up. "Beggin' the major's pardon, sir, but I've been runnin' jail coaches through these parts for a long while. I've met the man several times an' transported a lot of prisoners Dallas Handley's brought in. Most every sheriff in West Texas will vouch for him bein' a square bounty hunter who's lending a hand to clean lawbreakers out of Texas."

"Sergeant Burke's standing up for you is good enough for me," the major said, running a nervous hand through his beard. "But if the Apache really did attack the way station and kill those innocent folks, that could spell big trouble for all of us." He motioned to a scowling old Indian with leathery features who was sitting in a chair by the window calmly smoking a pipe. The heavy chains that were attached to steel manacles around his wrists and ankles rattled whenever the stoic, venerable Apache moved.

Omar Lassiter took a thoughtful sip of a cup of tepid coffee. "I heard that Geronimo here had surrendered. After that happening I would wonder why any of his tribe would wipe out a way station. That does not seem a prudent move on their part to secure either his safety or his release."

Dallas and his father looked at each other, thunderstruck. Barney said, "Are you tellin' us that old Indian's Geronimo? Hell's bells, I'd have expected an entire company of troops to be escorting his hide. That feller's more slippery than a greased eel."

Geronimo fixed Barney in his gaze. The Apache's dark eyes were like bits of obsidian. His expression betrayed no emotion when he spoke in surprisingly good English. "This is the fourth time I have surrendered. It will be my last. The Army could never catch me, but they did my People. A man's place is with his People, so now I am in chains and going to Florida. I hear it never snows there. That will be something to behold."

Major Green said, "We're transporting him in secret to Fort Stockton, where he'll be put on a train with the rest of his tribe. General Cook thought this might stop some of the young bucks who want to keep on fighting from breaking him out. The sooner he's on that train for Florida, the better it will be for all of us."

"My word," Omar Lassiter said thoughtfully, "Geronimo in person. What a draw he would be for our circus."

Jack Hanson, who ran the way station, snorted. "It'd be a glad day to attend that bastard's hanging. That sentiment would also go for most folks who've had family butchered by him."

Sergeant Burke spun an empty coffee cup. "Jack's brother got killed by a band of Apache over in Arizona Territory a few years back."

The chains on Geronimo's hands clinked when he gave a dismissive gesture. "Many, many of my People, women and children, have been murdered by the white eyes. I have done no wrong without cause, but now we are going to Florida where it never snows, and will kill no more."

"From what we just heard happened to the Jenson family at that way station," Jack Hanson boomed, "I'd say the only redskin to be trusted is a dead one."

Geronimo turned to stare out the window at the elephants. "That was the work of white eyes. No Indian kills horses, we steal them instead. They are valuable."

"The Apache is right," Dallas said. "We've been trailing Tiberius Poxon and Harry Latts since Devil's Gate. Those two are as easy to follow as a telegraph line. There's no doubt in my mind who committed that massacre."

Barney added, "And we're of the mind that if all of these cavalry men hadn't shown up, those cussed scalawags would've rubbed out everyone here too. They know we're on their trail. Keepin' us from fresh horses an' water will slow us down maybe enough for them to make a getaway."

Sergeant Burke lit a cigarette. "El Paso or any big city's a great place to disappear. Mexico's right across the Rio Grande River. But then they could just take a train an' be most anywheres in short order. Hard to believe how fast folks can move about these days. Trains travel up to thirty miles an hour. Now, that's covering some ground."

"I robbed a train once," Geronimo said idly, still staring

out at the elephants. No one at the table paid him any mind.

"So you are saying"—Major Green forked a piece of apple pie about on his plate—"that the two fugitives you're after were planning to attack this station, kill everyone and everything here, simply to slow you two down. I find that difficult to believe."

"With all due respect, Major," Dallas said, leaning back in his chair, "look over that way station tomorrow morning and bury the dead. Then, I believe you'll take a different outlook on Poxon and Latts. They're evil an' black-hearted as sin itself."

Jack Hanson shook his burly body like a wet dog when he snorted at Dallas. "You're a damn liar. The Apache killed all those people, if'n they actually were kilt. All we got to go by is your say-so, an' I ain't giving any damn liar fresh horses to go catch people for money. I reckon a bullet's more what you need."

"Simmer down, Mr. Hanson." Major Green slammed a fist on the table hard enough to upset a salt shaker. "Any more talk like that and I'll slap you in irons and chain you to Geronimo."

Sergeant Burke scooted back from the table. He had seen a glint in the way station operator's dark eyes that spoke of unreasoning hatred and a killing mood, a mix that was almost always a guarantee of bloodshed.

Hanson's chair flew back with a crash. "Damn you all, first I'll kill you bounty hunter, then that murdering red—"

Dallas had his hand on his Colt and was preparing to fire through the table at his adversary when he noticed Hanson freeze as if he were a mannequin whose mainspring had broken. Then Dallas noticed a stream of crimson beginning to drop from where a knife had come from nowhere to stick through the man's gunhand.

"The hell?" Hanson appeared dazed as he stumbled back.

Omar Lassiter held another knife at the ready. He said very calmly, "One of my circus acts is a knife-throwing demonstration. I suggest, my good sir, that you allow me to recover my property, then have your wife bandage your hand. Should you persist in such a vicious trend of behavior, my next knife will go into the hollow of your throat and go on to sever your spinal cord. I assure you this *will* happen."

"I'm not your enemy," Dallas said to Hanson, keeping his .45 at the ready. "And believe me, there's already been plenty of killing in these parts. I'd favor you settling down. Your wife needs a husband and your kids needs a daddy. The choice is yours."

Jack Hanson's eyes glazed. The big man slowly crumpled to the floor in a dead faint.

Sergeant Burke bent and grabbed the pistol from Hanson's holster. "Havin' family killed sometimes causes folks to act rash. I've known Jack for a spell, an' he ain't generally prone to this type of behavior. I reckon seein' ole Geronimo in the flesh kinda caused him to become unhinged in the head."

"He's lucky to have lived through going crazy," Dallas said, holstering his Colt.

Omar Lassiter went over and recovered his knife, then wrapped Hanson's bleeding hand tight with a handkerchief. He gave the blood-smeared blade an annoyed look, then proceeded to the sink basin to wash it clean. "I'm gratified he'll only have a sore hand to deal with. I threw the knife to go in sideways so it would miss the bones and minimize the damage."

A wide-eyed private who had remained in a corner of the room said in obvious awe to Lassiter, "I never saw anyone move as fast as you did. Could you really have hit him in the Adam's apple?"

The circus owner gave a thin grin. "An inch below the Adam's apple actually. The blade has to go in deep enough to chop the man's spine in two. This always brings about a quick kill, without allowing them to make another move that could fire a gun."

"Jeez." The soldier shook his head in disbelief and repeated. "I never saw anyone more so dang *fast.*"

"Now that that's over and no one is badly hurt," Major Green said, retaking his seat at the table, "I propose we accept, on my sergeant's word, that the Handleys here are telling us the truth when they claim to be honestly in hot pursuit of a pair of murderers. And that also a terrible slaughter has not only occurred at the next way station, but that also one was narrowly avoided here by our timely arrival."

"Glad to hear you makin' some sense finally," Barney said, mouthing a long-dead stub of cigar. "Ain't all that common in the Army, or at least it weren't back when I was servin' in it."

The major grinned. "I thought you had a military bearing about you, Mr. Handley. I'm also betting you were an officer in the Confederacy."

"Artillery officer, made the rank of captain before General Lee finally ran out of ammunition an' men to fight with."

Major Green decided there had already been enough upset without mentioning he had been a young officer fighting on General Ulysses S. Grant's side of the war. "I'm sure you were an excellent artilleryman."

Barney caught himself before admitting that he had just enjoyed some recent practice of his skills by blowing up a mansion. Some folks took dim views of things like that, especially when they were not there at the time and able to understand his good reasoning. "Thanks, Major," was all he said.

Dallas said in a somber tone, "We need fresh horses and, if you can spare it, some jerky or pemmican. There are several other way stations between here and El Paso. I fear those two will continue slaughtering innocent people simply to slow us down."

Sergeant Burke said, "Major, I'm of the mind a few of our boys should go along an' lend 'em a hand. Outlaws that'll slaughter women an' little kids an' poison water ain't fit to live."

"None of my People would poison water," Geronimo remarked. He was still staring out the window, transfixed by the elephants. But, surprisingly, the old warrior had not asked about what they were. "That is a bad thing indeed. I think I would kill these men." He hesitated. "But I am going to Florida."

Major Green motioned to Geronimo. "My orders are to get him to Fort Stockton. If it turned out that massacre was actually the work of the Apache, I'll need every man and every rifle in my troop. No, Sergeant, I will commandeer fresh horses for our bounty hunters and supply them with what rations we can spare, but that is all."

"Thanks, Major," Dallas said. "That's about all anyone can do under the circumstances." He sighed. "We had best be going. There's plenty of light to pick up their trail. I'm fairly sure they were hiding in those rocks south of here, watching you when you rode in."

"If those bastards keep up their dirty tricks," Barney said with a sigh, "this could turn back into a thirsty and tedious manhunt. Maybe you could spare us a few canteens to carry water for our horses."

"There are some gallon-sized ones on the prison wagon," Major Green said agreeably. "Take all you can pack. I'll do what I can to help you men catch up with those murderers."

Omar Lassiter had cleaned the blood from his knife and returned it to a hidden row of sheaths that had been sewn inside his bright red jacket. "I believe we should call the womenfolk back in. Mr. Hanson's hand is still leaking blood, I see. It should be dressed." The bald man turned to Dallas and his father. "My purse is becoming quite depleted. Devil's Gate was a washout, as you know. Perhaps, for a moderate piece of the reward money for those two, I could offer my assistance."

Barney said, "There ain't no doubt about you bein' mighty good with a knife, but if'n Dallas an' me gets close enough to stab 'em, I'd venture they'll already be bleedin' from a whole bunch of bullet holes we'll have put in their worthless hides."

Omar gave a nod to the elephants that had captivated Geronimo's attention. "No, Mr. Handley, what I have in mind is something totally different."

Chapter 23

Butch Conroy looked up from a pot of pinto beans and red chilies that were simmering in a cast-iron Dutch oven over his campfire to study the two men who were riding toward his camp.

From his first impression, they were dressed like white men. Most likely cowboys or prospectors like himself. Mexican bandits were always a problem anywhere along the border, but in the light of a full moon he could see the strangers were not Mexicans, so he only shifted his old Navy Colt to a more accessible position on his lanky hips. A lone man in wild lonesome country of the Devil Ridge mountains in far West Texas could ill afford to be *too* trusting.

Conroy, at a silver fifty-four years of age, had not survived as a single-blanket, jackass prospector for all of those years without taking reasonable precautions, yet he knew full well the delight of running across a camp with a hot meal to share, along with having someone to talk to. Briefly he tried to remember exactly how long it had been since he had had a human being to visit with. One-way conversations with ol' Useless, his burro, were becoming tiresome. It had to have been well over six months.

The newcomers might even bring word of a new strike. Butch was ready to pull foot from this barren country without a lot of urging. He had tried dry-panning every wash and chipping samples from any outcrop that might possibly contain paydirt for more than a year without success. Yet he knew any strike that would be rich enough to make him rich would sadly never be found close to a town with a decent saloon. Becoming a wealthy mining magnate such as Tiberius Poxon down in Devil's Gate had managed to do took determination along with the patience of Job.

"Hello the camp," the slender man with long black hair spilling down his back from beneath a felt Bollinger hat hollered out from where the duo had halted at a mannerly distance.

Butch relaxed. "Welcome, strangers, tie up those horses of y'all's an' come on in. I've got a big pot of Mex beans about cooked up that'll feed us all." He decided to splurge. The handful of Arbuckle's coffee he had kept carefully stowed away, wrapped in muslin cloth in the bottom of his saddlebag, was being saved for company anyway. "An' later we'll boil us up a pot of coffee."

The two men nodded in unison and dismounted. A few moments later the smiling, well-dressed strangers were sitting across the flickering campfire from the old prospector.

"Harry Latts." The younger man reached around the fire and gave Butch a firm handshake. "Thank you for inviting us into your camp. Not too many folks these days are so trusting."

"Well, shucks," Butch Conroy said lifting the heavy lid to check on the progress of his beans. "I reckon most people are good when ya really get down to it, an' y'all look okay to me. Sharin' a camp out here's better for all of us. There's bandits an' Apache enough to keep a body on his toes without frettin' fellow prospectors."

The older of the two men, who wore a spiffy suit of clothes along with a black bowler, said, "The Apache are not going to be much of a problem any longer, now that Geronimo has surrendered."

Butch dropped the iron lid back onto the Dutch oven with a clang. "Now there's a good piece of news if I've ever heard one. Reckon if y'all know of a rich strike hereabouts, that'll make this day some pumpkins for sure, yep, yep. When did that red devil decide his butt had got whipped?"

"Several months ago, I'm not certain of the date." The unnamed man's silver hair glistened in the wan light of the killing moon. "Your beans smell quite good, I must say."

"Gotta have lots of peppers." The old prospector grinned to show his front teeth were missing. "Make it hot enough to burn the lint outta yer belly button an' you'll stay healthy as a goat, I'm here to tell ya."

Butch was feeling magnanimous. *These new friends might stay around and visit for a while in the morning,* he thought, and added, "Boys, I've got a dab of lard an' saleratus to mix with some flour for breakfast. Dutch oven biscuits are the best. Just too bad there ain't no honey to sweeten 'em with."

"I have some in my bag," the man called Harry Latts said agreeably. "I'll fetch it."

Butch started to yell at him that the honey wasn't needed until morning, but the young man had already faded into the night. Kids these days had no patience. He still had the older fellow to visit with, however. "I don't believe I caught your name, my friend."

"No, you didn't." The silver-haired man tilted back

his bowler and regarded him from across the low, flickering fire. "My name is Tiberius Poxon."

The old prospector bolted back, his eyes wide. "Not *the* same Poxon who owns all those rich silver mines down there in Devil's Gate?"

"Yes, sir." Poxon shifted to one side of the fire and extended a hand. "And I must say, I am very glad to make your acquaintance."

Butch Conroy started to reach out his hand, but strangely could not do so. Everything felt odd, it was as if he had no strength left in his body. For some reason he could not fathom, his neck was wet. This was queer, there wasn't a rain cloud in the sky. Then, when the old prospector looked down to see the front of his tattered shirt was awash in blood, he realized his throat had been cut from ear to ear. *No, this is all a bad dream, a nightmare, I'll wake up in a little bit and laugh about . . . wait a moment, I see a most wondrous light. I'll check that out first.*

Harry Latts gave the prospector a hard kick with a boot to keep the old man's body from falling into the fire, possibly upsetting the dinner.

"I could see no reason to waste a bullet on such a dolt."

"A correct assessment, Mr. Latts. Besides, sound travels *so* far in the desert, discretion is always wise." Poxon chuckled evilly. "And, thanks to you, he didn't spill the beans."

Latts ignored his boss's latest display of lunacy. "Too bad there is no water to spare. I detest not being able to clean my knife before replacing it into its sheath."

"We must all bear adversity on occasion, Mr. Latts, yet we learn from it. As the Bard so aptly wrote, 'Sweet are the uses of adversity; which like the toad, ugly and venomous, wears yet a precious jewel in its head.'"

Harry Latts stifled a snort of anger. He had no idea

who this Bard fellow was, nor did he understand any of that nonsense. His damn knife was bloody and he wanted to clean it, for Pete's sake, that was all.

"I'll check his bags for that coffee," Harry said. "We'll boil up a pot while we eat. Then I feel we should keep on moving."

"While you are over there with an already bloody knife, cut the burro's throat also."

"Yes, sir." Latts once again blended into the night like a fey spirit, moving about with no more noise than a slithering snake.

Tiberius Poxon stirred the beans, taking a taste to assure himself they were cooked to perfection. He gave a thin grin of satisfaction when he heard a brief, quickly stifled scream of pain and terror from the old fool's burro; then the silence of night in the desert returned.

"He had almost nothing of value, sir," Harry said, slamming a battered saddlebag onto the dry dirt near the flickering fire. "But the beans do smell good."

"Grab us some plates, Mr. Latts. I believe you will enjoy the repast. The pintos are nicely spiced, just as we both like them."

Latts fished out a couple of tin plates and handed one of them to his employer. "Lucky we ran across him. Otherwise, we'd have gone hungry."

"Ah, my dear Mr. Latts." Tiberius Poxon ladled out beans to the keening melodies of distant coyotes. "As it says in the Bible, good things *always* come to the deserving. One must strive to keep an optimistic attitude. I hold no doubts whatsoever that I shall return triumphant to Devil's Gate, where, after an appropriate show of force and the hiring of a new, more competent sheriff, I will once again reign as king of my own domain."

Maybe you should rebuild that mansion of yours out of stones, nice thick ones. Latts kept his thoughts to himself and took a healthy bite of steaming beans along with a generous hunk of red pepper. "I must say, sir, things seem to be looking up."

Another pack of coyotes joined in serenading the Apache moon that had grown in intensity to anoint the desert with an eerie yellow light. It reminded Tiberius Poxon of the coal-oil floodlights that illuminated the stage shows on riverboats along the Mississippi.

"I agree completely, Mr. Latts." Poxon smiled upon his steaming plate of beans. "I have a feeling that, finally, the Good Lord has smiled upon us and that things are beginning to come our way."

Chapter 24

Barney Handley sat beside Omar Lassiter on the high front seat of the lumbering circus wagon. Even though they had been on the road since before the crack of dawn, the old fellow kept smiling like a kid in a candy store after finding a silver dollar in the street.

Earlier, by the fiery orange light of a new day being born, Barney had plainly seen a small field mouse scurry from a clump of grass to run in front of the lead elephant. The huge beast had squashed the hapless rodent flatter than a boardinghouse pancake without hesitation. That was when he realized not everything he had heard about elephants was true. They certainly were not frightened by mice. Having an expert on pachyderms to learn from was an opportunity to be taken advantage of.

From the corner of his eye, Omar noticed Barney's mouth begin to open in what would surely be the hundredth question of the early morning about elephants. The old gentleman was simply curious. That was what drew people to a circus in the first place. But there Omar had ample opportunities to move on without offense. Being forced to sit alongside even a nice person who did nothing but ask endless questions was beginning to grate on his nerves, like fingernails being drawn along glass. Then, much to Omar's unexpressed delight, an idea flashed on inside his head.

"Barney, my friend," Omar said, "I'll bet you would enjoy riding on an elephant with Halim. Our driver was born in Madras, India, and is a trained mahout. Halim not only knows far more than I about them, but he also speaks quite good English."

"What's a 'mahoot'?" Barney asked, his gray eyebrows lowered in thought.

"The word is spelled m-a-h-o-u-t. In India it's simply a title given to someone who is quite proficient in the care, training, and working of elephants."

"That sounds like a man I'd want to talk with. You say he speaks English? I reckon I'm somewhat surprised at that. He sure don't dress like folks in Texas do."

Omar smiled cheerfully. "Barney, I guarantee you're going to be completely amazed."

After a brief stop to employ a stepladder, Barney Handley sat astride the lead elephant, directly behind Halim, his green eyes wide with awe. The mahout ignored his new passenger, keeping his focus on the jagged horizon. Once the stepladder had been stowed and everyone was on board once again, Halim lightly touched the lead elephant's massive forehead with the long stick that seemingly never left his hand, starting the gigantic wagon lumbering across the plains once again.

"Omar told me you speak some English," Barney said to Halim.

The mahout kept his gaze ahead. "Yeah, Boss, I got a fair handle on the subject." His accent was straight out of the Bronx.

Barney's already wide eyes opened even more. "You sure don't talk like you're from India."

"I was born there, Boss. My daddy's a doctor, has a big

banana plantation. I worked with elephants until I got old enough to go to college. Pap sent me to Fordham University in New York. I stayed there six years, studying the nightlife, then moved on to the day life. Pap became somewhat upset with my grades for some reason, and cut off my funding. Mr. Lassiter's circus was playing nearby, so I joined on to see the country. Jolly good times, or at least they were until we came to Texas."

"The place ain't so bad once you get used to it."

"I believe they say the same about carbuncles."

Barney decided to change the line of conversation. "Reckon you do know a lot about elephants."

"More than I care to, Boss. You think horses are messy to clean up after, try elephants. No one *ever* gives that matter any thought. And believe me, you don't want to be in the same barn with one when it breaks wind."

For some reason Barney felt a waning interest in elephants. Now that the huge beasts had been likened to overgrown horses, it tended to take away the glow, yet they were so *big*.

"Elephants have more stamina than a horse," Halim said without urging. "They can pull a heavy load like Lassiter's wagon—it weighs over five tons—for a full day in the hot sun without stopping for rest or water. Yeah, Boss, for a manhunt you can't beat 'em. Those dirty rats we're chasing after are going to get run to ground by us if they don't get mighty lucky."

Barney studied the distant horizon. "Ain't just plannin' on running them to ground; our plan is to put 'em under it."

"Ah, Boss, after what I heard those desperados did, you're preachin' to the choir."

"They're likely the worst there is."

"No, Boss, I'd say there's just as bad in India. The thuggees rob folks all the time, then strangle them with a short rope. They're where the word 'thug' in the dictionary came from. A bloody rotten bunch of buggers those thuggees are, and thicker than fleas on an elephant."

Barney's interest in elephants slid another notch lower. Fleas were a much more urgent subject than thugs in India. "Elephants get infested with fleas?"

"Yeah, Boss, it's how the fleas get around. All the more work for me. I have to keep them dusted down with a mixture of stove ash, a dash of quicklime along with a dab of potassium permanganate. That generally keeps the itchy little buggers under control, leastwise when it ain't rainin'. Then's when you got troubles, let me tell you."

Barney Handley found himself learning far more about the huge gray beasts than he wanted to know. "Tell me more about those thuggees."

"Sure, Boss, but there's a lot more to caring for elephants that you need to know. For one thing they stay pregnant for two years, an' I'll tell you, when it's mating season you sure have to stay on your toes around 'em."

Barney fished a cigar from his vest and fired it. The day was shaping up to be another long one.

"I must say, this circus wagon is something to behold." Dallas Handley was riding inside the swaying coach with Omar's wife, Princess Noria. He decided that studying the woodwork might help keep his gaze from the beautiful lady, whose trim bare midriff and enticing figure was an attraction not to be easily denied.

"Omar had it custom-built in South Bend, Indiana, by the Studebaker Company. He calls it a 'traveling home.'" Noria batted her turquoise eyelids. "Let me show you some of the features."

Dallas didn't trust his voice not to falter, so he simply nodded to the stunningly beautiful woman.

"Here is our bath." Noria opened a mahogany door to show not only a built-in washbasin with gold fixtures, but a bathtub and, of all things, an oak water closet. She noted the amazement in Dallas's eyes. "There are water tanks overhead, and another tank underneath that can be dumped whenever necessary." Noria chuckled. "Usually outside of town."

"Convenient," Dallas mumbled.

"Oh, don't be so shy, Mr. Handley. A circus has to attract attention, and so do the performers. I don't dress like this to have men ignore me. My husband is on the observation deck and he knows I am completely loyal to him."

Dallas said, "Yes, ma'am, I'll do my best, but we don't have a lot of women in Texas that'll show a bare belly in public. Kinda takes me aback."

"Just remember, it's all part of a show. We left the rest of our troop in Denver when we came to scout out the West for possible circus appearances. As Omar has said, Texas seems to be a washout."

"This wagon isn't the whole shebang?"

"Oh, no, we have nearly a hundred performers, lions, tigers, trained bears, high-wire walkers, trapeze artists. You name it and Lassister's traveling circus has it."

"Observation deck?" The concept had just sunk in. "What's that, Princess?"

She gave a musical chuckle. "Since we will be traveling together, I believe it's time to drop the show-business facade. My real name is Mabel Washburn, and I'm from Chicago. My husband was born Frank Smith in Davenport, Iowa. His family has always been undertakers; needless to say they are quite unhappy with Omar's occupation."

"I've got a lot to learn about being in show business."

"The first thing to remember is, everything's an illusion. Give people an opportunity to dream, see new things. Then fleece the suckers out of every dollar you can."

"The observation deck?" Dallas repeated, staring at the lady's daringly cut deerskin halter top that was delightfully filled to overflowing. He swallowed and added, "Missus Lassiter."

With another musical chuckle she reached for a knotted rope dangling from the ceiling. "Call me Mabel, all my friends do." With a firm pull, a rectangle-shaped door came open on a hinge, displaying a folding ladder, which the lady quickly laid out and made ready to climb. "After you," she said with a wave of a hand that displayed long pink fingernails upon which delicate butterflies had been painstakingly painted.

"Ma'am." Dallas nodded. He reluctantly pulled his gaze from the shapely lass and climbed up through the opening to stand atop the huge, lumbering coach. A scant moment later, Mabel stood beside him, her rosebud perfume still heady, even in the open air.

A brass railing about four feet high surrounded the sides of the wagon, save an opening to the front seat, where Omar Lassiter was sitting. The circus owner smiled at his wife, then stood and came to join them.

"I only sit there to keep from upsetting folks," Omar said. "Actually, the reins running from the wagon to the harnesses are simply for show. Halim guides and controls the elephants using touches from his wand. Few people realize just how smart and docile these huge animals actually are when treated well. Compared to horses, they are gentle as lambs."

Dallas gave a grin when he noticed his father riding behind Halim on the lead elephant. "Your wife has been filling me in on the circus business. It's something we generally don't learn much about here in West Texas. But I must say, it looks like Dad's having fun."

"That's the reason circuses exist, my bounty hunter friend." Omar offered Dallas one of the thin black cigars he carried a seemingly endless supply of inside his red jacket. "We sell only the opportunity to leave the drabness of day-to-day existence and experience new and wondrous things. For a quite reasonable fee, I must add."

"I think that is great." Dallas bent to allow Omar to light his cigar with what appeared to be a solid gold lighter with a huge diamond embedded in its side. "Living out on the frontier is a rather boring proposition, unless there's outlaws or Indians about."

Omar held his lighter to sparkle in the bright sunshine. "Cheap bronze with a chunk of glass. A bit of showman chicanery, or part of the entertainment. This manhunt we have joined you on is quite real. I must say I find it oddly thrilling after making my living by amusing people for a lot of years."

"At least, my dear," Mabel said cheerfully, "you will gain an adventure to tell others when we return to civilization."

"You are correct there, dear. Even my nemesis, Phineas Barnum, most certainly has not had the good fortune to join in a genuine manhunt. The quarry here is most challenging, most challenging indeed."

Dallas was aghast. "You agreed to help us because you thought it would be fun!"

"Along with possibly of helping regain some of our expense money. Using short shrift, yes. I have always enjoyed a jolly good hunt. Having the opportunity to pursue the deadliest of all species is an experience not to be missed."

Dallas mumbled, "Just like your wife said, everything about show business is an illusion."

"Ah, quite correct, my bounty hunter friend. I may possibly even come up with an act for my circus employing some of the thrilling elements of a Western manhunt."

Dallas puffed on his cigar in hopes of calming his raging temper. The bald showman was using the pursuit of a pair of the bloodiest murderers and rapists he had ever encountered as *entertainment*. The coldness of the man was beyond comprehension. Then, through the rising heat waves from the desert floor, against the glare of an azure sky, he could plainly see a thin column of dark smoke rising from the horizon straight ahead.

"Well, Mr. Lassiter," Dallas said icily, pointing to the wisp of smoke with his thin cigar, "I'm saying in a short while you can leave those illusions behind for your performances. In my line of work, death is dirty and bloody. And folks don't get shot, then get up, dust themselves off, and walk away once the show's over. They're killed and they stay that way."

"Dear," Mabel said, her voice tense, "are there going to be actual dead people?"

"I . . . I hope not," Omar stuttered.

"You were mighty correct about one thing," Dallas said.

"What's that?" Omar asked, staring now at the distant spire of smoke.

"The quarry we're after is challenging. And Tiberius Poxon and Harry Latts are getting more skilled at killing all the time. Remember to respect them like the various animals they are, or you might not live to tell of *this* experience."

Chapter 25

Sarah Taylor was in a joyous mood. Today she was celebrating her eighth birthday. When the little girl saw the dust the two riders were making as they headed toward her daddy's way station, she squealed with delight. Having company come calling was a wonderful thing. There were no other children for her to play with for miles. Being an only child, Sarah often felt lonely, especially during holidays or on a special occasion like today.

Maybe the visitors will stay long enough to have a piece of my birthday cake, she thought as she ran to the pallid frame house where she had lived with her parents the past two long years. Her mama, Laurie, had baked a big chocolate cake and it tasted so good. Ice cream would be great to go with it, but that could only happen on rare occasions in the wintertime when enough snow could be gathered. No matter, the approaching strangers would almost certainly enjoy sharing her wonderful birthday cake.

"Howdy, gents," her father, George, greeted the men with his usual smile. "Shapin' up to be another hot one, for sure. Tie your horses to water, then come in an' rest for a spell. We have a treat for y'all." He nodded to Sarah, causing her to blush. "It's my daughter's birthday an' Ma's baked up a chocolate cake. Maybe you'd enjoy a piece to go with a cup of coffee."

"Why, that sounds simply scrumptious," the older of the two men said as he dismounted. "I'm sure all the kids are enjoying a birthday party."

"George Taylor," the stage stop operator said offering a hand. "That's one of the problems of livin' out like this. There ain't any kids closer than the Hansons to the east. Ma and me's only been blessed with Sarah."

"Well, my, my," the younger man said as he came to Sarah wearing a beaming smile. "Come over here to Harry Latts. I'll bet I've got a real good surprise for our little birthday girl."

Sarah looked to her father for permission. He gave a nod of approval, sending the little girl running and giggling to Latts.

Tiberius Poxon noticed a woman approaching from the house. She wore a plain print dress. Her leathery, lined face spoke of years of toil beneath the relentless desert sun.

"And this must be Sarah's mother," Poxon said, his voice cheery. "I'm sorry we are the only ones to show up for the girl's party."

"Don't be, sir," Laurie Taylor said. "I'm sure we will make a grand time of it." She grasped his hand. "Living out like this, we're always grateful for company. Laurie Taylor's my name. I believe you've already met my husband George."

"Yes, ma'am. You folks can call me Tiberius."

"My, how wonderful. Being named after the famous Roman emperor, Tiberius Caesar Augustus, is quite exceptional. Your family must have expected great things from you."

"Oh, yes," Tiberius Poxon said, a surprised and wistful look on his face, "and I have not been a disappointment.

I must say I am truly amazed to encounter such an educated person as yourself here in such a remote place as this."

Laurie mimicked his wistful look. "I graduated from Iowa Teachers College with a major in Latin. Then I met George and fell in love." She sighed. "A person never knows what course the fates will charter."

"No, Missus Taylor, they do not. I would very much like to continue this most delightful conversation, but as the Bard so aptly put it in Julius Caesar, 'There is a tide in the affairs of men which, taken at the flood, leads on to fortune.' This is in Act Four, if I remember correctly. Now, sadly, we must be about our affairs, for the dogs of war are nipping at our very heels."

Laurie Taylor bolted back, fear in her eyes. "You men are wanted by the law!"

Tiberius Poxon drew his pistol with a smooth, easy motion and without hesitation shot her through the heart. He said as she slumped to the dry Texas earth, "How perceptive of you, my dear. I never like to kill an educated person, but . . ." He swung around and planted a bullet square in the middle of George Taylor's back as the man ran toward the open door of the way station. "To quote the Bard once again, 'There's a time for all things.'"

Harry Latts held the terrified young girl with an arm to her throat so tight she could only muster a gurgle. "Sir," he said, "I believe I should take her behind the station house. Another 'Indian' raid will be more convincing."

Poxon shrugged. "Finish with her as quickly as possible, Mr. Latts. Then, after we have had our lunch, we must destroy this place and be on our way."

Latts said as he grabbed up Sarah, "I will join you shortly." Then, already ripping the dress from the struggling girl, he disappeared behind the gray wood station house.

Tiberius Poxon gave the body of Laurie Taylor one last, long look. "'Tis pity you cannot hear one more time the words of Shakespeare; his writings are appropriate to all occasions. 'Sigh no more, ladies, sigh no more, men are deceivers ever, one foot in sea and one on shore; to one thing constant never.'"

Poxon gave an empty chuckle. "Death lies on her like an untimely frost." Then he went inside the way station to enjoy a nice big piece of chocolate cake.

Chapter 26

"The buzzards are pecking on the body of an old feller that had his throat cut," Dallas Handley said when he came back and climbed inside the circus wagon. They had decided to make a brief stop on their way to the distant column of smoke to check out a thick circling of vultures not far off the road. "They also killed the man's burro. Most likely that poor guy was paid a visit by Poxon and Latts sometime last night, by the looks of it."

"How awful," Mabel Washburn said, wrinkling her nose. "We really must bury him; it's the only decent thing to do."

Barney had taken advantage of the stop to return to the coach. He had learned far more about elephants than he ever wanted to know. "With all due respect, ma'am, we can't take the time."

"All my wife is asking," Omar Lassiter said, "is for us to display the milk of human kindness. No honorable man leaves another of his brethren to be devoured as carrion by birds."

"You fancy yourself a hunter," Dallas said sharply. "The most vicious wild animals of your worst nightmare pale beside those two desperados. They're smart too. If they succeed in slowing us down by causing us to bury folks, they'll get plumb away and most likely never be punished for any of this. How do you feel about honorable men *not* doing everything in their power to save others? Poxon and Latts are worse then mad dogs on the loose."

Omar gave a sigh of resignation and turned to his wife. "I am sorry, my dear, but our bounty hunter friend's logic is inescapable. And the hunt is everything." He stuck his head out the window. "Take us ahead, Halim, with all possible speed."

"Got ya, Boss." With a firm touch of his wand to the lead elephant's forehead, the mahout started the huge wagon lumbering once again across the dusty plain.

It took nearly two hours for them to traverse the barren expanse to the source of the smoke. The circus owner and his wife expressed a combination of dismay and anger over the delay. The Handleys, with long experience as to how the desert can distort distance, stoically puffed on cigars while keeping an eagle eye on their surroundings. No one ever rushed in the waterless wastelands, especially in the heat of the day, which was increasingly gripping the desert with a fiery hand.

"How do they know?" Omar Lassiter motioned to myriad black vultures circling what they now recognized as a burned-out way station. "It's eerie how they can sense death so quickly."

"That's one mystery no one can explain," Barney said, squinting into the bright, cloudless sky. "Most believe they are attracted by the smell of blood, but I've known folks to fall off a horse and break their necks, or sometimes just die a natural death, yet the buzzards were on 'em like stink on . . ." He gave Mabel a sheepish glace. "Uh—uh—a cowplop."

Dallas said, "An old Apache medicine man, who was in jail over in Fort Stockton, told me that the departing spirits of the dead, both man and animal, call to the birds to welcome them to their earthly remains. He explained that all spirits are happy being with the Great Gods in the Happy Hunting Ground of the next world. They do not want to return to their bodies and call to the birds to prevent the possibility."

"Heathen beliefs," Omar said. "I believe they sense death, how I don't know, they just do."

"One things for certain," Dallas said. "There's been some departed spirits leave *this* way station. Now that we're pulling up to it, let's go see if there's anything to be done."

Halim was the first to let out a wail of grief. The skinny little man agilely scurried down a rope from the elephant's saddle. He stood in the hot sun, his wand tucked beneath an arm, studying the scene of death and destruction with a grim face. "Terrible, terrible, Boss. I've never seem the like," he said aloud to no one. "In the name of all gods, this is awful."

The door of the circus wagon swung open. Dallas and his father jumped out, weapons at the ready, followed by the wide-eyed circus owner and his wife.

"They're getting tired," Dallas said, staring grimly at the bodies of a man and woman lying on the barren ground in front of the smoldering remains of the stage stop. "The last way station they destroyed, all the bodies were dragged inside and burnt"—he hesitated—"most of them anyway."

"There has to be over two dozen dead horses in that corral," Omar said, his eyes narrow slits. "Whoever did this are worse than barbarians."

"Never heard of that tribe before," Barney said. "But Indians surely don't kill horses." The old artilleryman looked sadly at the pathetically small, naked body of what he knew would be a very young girl that was draped over a large rock behind the smoldering remains of the building. "No Apache did that either. They take captives, but they don't rape and slaughter like what happened here."

Dallas lowered the hammer on his Winchester. There was not even a wounded animal to put out of its misery. The only sound was the low keening of a hot, dry desert wind fanning the embers of wanton devastation. The myriad buzzards circling overhead against a blue sky completed the picture of a bloody massacre of innocents.

"Let's see if they left us their calling card." Barney turned and headed for the low rock water tank beside a heap of burnt rubble that had been a wooden windmill. Dallas explained as the trio followed. "At the last station Poxon and Latts destroyed, those two dumped dead dogs and coal oil in the tank to poison it and keep us from watering our horses to slow us down."

Barney stood staring blankly down into the low circle of rocks. When the others joined him, they saw the reason for his shock. Floating in coal-oil-polluted water was the body of a puppy. There was a white ribbon with HAPPY BIRTHDAY written on it tied around the dog's neck.

Mabel began to shiver, choking back sobs of grief. Omar forced his gaze from the dead puppy to the small body draped over a rock.

"Those bastards are worse than any wild animal could ever be," the circus owner spit. He walked around the smoldering ruins of the way station to stand and look down forlornly at the savaged little girl. Tears streaked his cheeks as he took off his fine red showman's jacket and tenderly wrapped it around her cold corpse.

Omar Lassiter picked up the slight burden and held her tenderly in his arms. His eyes were dark pinpoints of wrath when he gave pantherlike screams of rage to the firmaments. After a long while, he grew silent. Omar carried the girl to the coach and gently placed her inside. He dabbed at his teary eyes with a white handkerchief, then rejoined his companions. "I will see to it she gets a Christian burial." He glared across the desert. "And I promise not to rest until the ones who did this are rotting in Hell."

Dallas nodded his agreement. The chubby circus owner wasn't such a bad sort after all. It would be nice to have a man burning with honorable rage helping them. Tiberius Poxon and Harry Latts could not be too far ahead now. His, and everyone else's, hope was to kill them before they could continue their outrages. Wordless vows of revenge were exchanged as all five gathered to heap rocks over the slain couple before continuing their trek of deadly vengeance.

Chapter 27

Harry Latts wore a worried brow when he rode behind his employer as they made their dusty way along the stage road heading for El Paso. Having Tiberius Poxon at his back gave him an increasing sense of unease. The man had always tended to be eccentric, but then so were most men who had carved out a fortune in the turbulent West.

Tiberius Poxon, however, was beginning to show all of the traits of a genuine lunatic. The quoting of some oddball poet call "The Bard" or another named Shakespeare was bad enough; none of the long drawn-out ramblings made the slightest sense. When Poxon began to use verses from the Bible to justify killing people and animals, Latts realized the hinges holding his mind in place were rapidly becoming unstuck.

Harry's own uncle had been "saved" by a traveling stump preacher when he was a lad of fifteen back in Missouri. Rufus Latts took to quoting Scripture and reading the Good Book from morning until night. Then he began speaking in tongues, which was really spooky.

Rufus kept ranting and raving about how he was on God's own mission to save souls from perdition, yet he never left the farmhouse. Harry's father said it would just be a matter of time until he got over it and went back to what had been his normal routine of drinking moonshine and playing cards, but that wasn't what happened. Not by a long shot.

Harry had been awakened one stormy night by what sounded like someone chopping wood. Only the rhythmic hacking was coming from his parents bedroom. He had been warned many times to never enter that room, but this time the door was open.

Vividly, oh, so vividly, Harry Latts remembered wrapping himself with a thick wool robe and going to see what the ruckus was about. By the light of a single flickering candle, he watched in horror as his Uncle Rufus, wielding a long corn knife, hacked again and again at the bloody bodies of his father and mother.

Sinners! The wages of sin is death! Rufus shouted over and over, as if by rote, chopping away with that bloody knife like an automaton.

Harry had run from the house unnoticed by his crazed uncle. The sheriff and deputy found Rufus still flailing away with the corn knife. They disarmed him, shackled him securely, and threw him in jail. Later, the addle-brained judge sent his uncle to some insane asylum. That was a crock. He should have been hanged for killing his family.

Not only had his lunatic uncle slaughtered his parents, but also his three brothers and two sisters, whose bodies were found lying in their beds with their heads lopped off.

Harry Latts had been thrust adrift to make his own hard way in the world by the cruel actions of a crazy man who quoted Scripture, just like Tiberius Poxon was beginning to do. A worrisome situation. But not one he couldn't handle. Harry had learned his survival skills from some of the best in the business.

Stunned by the tragic demise of his family, Harry drifted aimlessly west, eventually coming to the booming cattle town of Wichita, Kansas. The devastated fifteen-year-old luckily found employment working as a swamper in a combination saloon and whorehouse run by Rowdy Joe Lowe and his gorgeous young blond wife, Kathryn, who was called Rowdy Kate by nearly all of their customers.

Rowdy Joe took a liking to the young boy and began to teach him to use a gun and knife when needed; skills often employed in a cattle town. Seldom did a night pass without at least one disgruntled customer being given a severe beating for complaining about being cheated out of money. Should anyone persist in being a nuisance, either Joe or Kate, who both wore twin pistols, would simply pull a gun and shoot the troublemaker dead.

Soon, Joe began to trust Harry well enough to let him handle problems. At the age of sixteen, he killed his first man, a drunken cowboy who was determined to have his way with Kate instead of one of the working girls upstairs that were readily available. The man was an obvious lunatic. When the lout pulled a knife, Harry shot him square in the throat.

Rowdy Joe and Kate were both very proud of him. Joe gave him a five-dollar bonus, telling him that if he was careful in the future to shoot someone where they wouldn't bleed all over the floor, the pay would go to ten dollars. Kate gave him a free hour with a young Indian girl in Room Thirteen. Strange how after all of this time he could remember the number of the room, but not the girl's name, nor what she looked like.

No matter. After a couple more years and a dozen dead men, Rowdy Joe himself got shot and killed in

Denver, where he had gone on business. Kate, oddly, seemed totally unmoved by the happening. She quietly sold the saloon and moved away to San Francisco, where, story has it, she married a wealthy mining magnate who coincidentally had numerous business interests in Denver.

Educated now in deceit, treachery, and murder, Harry began working as a hired gun. After an especially messy set of circumstances in Spokane, Washington, Harry had felt it prudent to spend some time in Canada. While there he had become depleted of funds and robbed a mail train, only slightly wounding the conductor. This was the only act he ever committed for which he had run afoul of the law. In the West, if any man he shot had a gun on their person, no sheriff ever pursued the matter; that made it plainly a case of self-defense.

The Canadians, however, held a more narrow view of train robbers, causing him to head south with all possible dispatch. It had been upon his arrival in Texas that he had learned of the rich silver strikes near Devil's Gate and come to be in the employ of Tiberius Poxon.

Now that Poxon was becoming a lunatic, it would soon be time to move on once again. The contents of his boss's saddlebags kept creeping into the forefront of his thoughts. Perhaps, if the man simply disappeared, Harry could keep his hard-won reputation, yet become rich. It was something to consider.

Briefly, Harry Latts pondered how he could fret over appearing honest to others, yet kill children with impunity. *Strange,* he thought, *I can't even remember what the little girl looked like, and that was mere hours ago. Hell, I can't remember what* any *of them looked like. It's a blessing really.*

Glancing occasionally at Tiberius Poxon's bulging

saddlebags, Harry Latts rode on toward El Paso entertaining the possibility of a rich future.

A very rich future indeed.

Tiberius Poxon kept reflecting back on the recent events in his town of Devil's Gate and wondering exactly what he had done so wrong as to cause him to flee. Running was not his style. Never had been.

Raised on Mississippi paddle-wheel showboats by his professional gambler father, Tiberius had barely known his mother. She was a whore anyway, or so his father, Augustus, had claimed. There was no denying the fact that she had abandoned him at a tender age to be raised on riverboats plying to the rough, deceitful, and often deadly gambling business along the lawless Mississippi. Not the actions of a decent Christian woman. Not by a long shot.

His mother's name was Sibyl, after Sibyl of Cumae, no doubt. That explained much; being named after a familiar of the underworld. No woman, however, could be trusted. Neither could any man, or so his father had taught.

To this day, the deep red scars of learning that crisscrossed his back and hips from his father's whippings were vivid reminders of the folly of trusting. Tiberius Poxon had learned his lessons well. Too well for his sweet father's own good. After recovering from a particularly savage whipping when he was only thirteen, Tiberius had taken an ice pick from his daddy's jacket—Augustus always believed in carrying an abundance of protection. His dear sweet father lay on his bed, snoring fitfully from consuming too much evil drink. Tiberius had felt a wave of utter pleasure, better than sex, when he shoved that ice pick into his sleeping father's ear with all of his might.

The besotted gambler had shivered like a clubbed fish for several minutes before growing eternally still. There were only a few drops of blood to clean up before sobbing to the captain that his daddy wouldn't wake up. The fools believed him. Called his father's death a stroke.

That was how a person got ahead in this world. Deceit, backed up by overwhelming force. Never show weakness. Never show compassion. Take what you can. Take it any way you must.

Yes, Tiberius reflected, his father *had* taught him well.

He was simply suffering a temporary setback due to a careless lack of displaying an iron hand in his hold over Devil's Gate. His town. Stolen fair and square from the weak fools who had found the riches, yet were too stupid to make the most of their God-given opportunities.

Where he had gone wrong was trusting too much. Sinker Wilson was an obvious idiot. Yet he'd allowed the man to buy those cannons. Should have hung him when he brought up the subject. Then his wonderful mansion would still be standing.

That bounty hunter who started things going wrong should have been hung the moment he rode into Devil's Gate. Been good for business. Hangings were always profitable. His saloon alone made a thousand dollars when Sinker had hung the whore. That was more money than any woman was worth.

The Good Book admonished, "Love is the fulfilling of the law." Tiberius Poxon loved his town. Loved his rich mines. Loved his beautiful mansion. And he would soon return to prove himself worthy of the charge. Once he regained control of his empire he would show more love for the law. Hang more whores and evildoers. That had been his failing; being too soft. His travails with the bounty hunter were a lesson from God. A lesson as painful as a buggy whip wielded by a drunken gambler.

Yes, Poxon vowed, he would return, lesson learned, to Devil's Gate. The titles to all of the mines and hard-stolen properties were safely stowed inside his saddle-bags. So was more cash than a dozen sinners ever earn in their wasted lifetimes.

Yes, people *were* dying for his cause. But the killings were ordained by God. The Book of Matthew plainly stated: "He that loseth his life for *my* sake shall find it." Words spoken by the Lord were law. And Tiberius Poxon loved the law.

The biggest question plaguing him was how to dispose of Harry Latts once they were safely in El Paso. It had to appear to be an accident. Or maybe a nice, explainable stroke.

Tiberius Poxon urged his fresh horse into a faster gait to the west. He was smiling now. All decent hotels furnished buckets of ice.

And nice sharp ice picks along with them.

Chapter 28

"Well, now, ain't this a fine kettle of fish." Barney stood atop the creaking circus wagon staring with obvious disdain at a huge gathering of black storm clouds rolling in quickly from the north. "Folks out here have likely been hoping for a good rain for years; just too dang bad it picked this time to hit. I'm betting this big wagon's gonna mire down in the mud like God's own anvil."

"The road seems to be mostly rock," Omar said hopefully, studying the ground ahead.

"You're not familiar with a cloudburst in the desert," Dallas said. "Every draw and low point can run water ten feet deep. And I mean swift water. I've seen an entire herd of cattle washed away, tumbling like toys. While we're on solid ground here, you need to consider there's also stretches of road that'll turn into some of the slickest mud in creation."

Not far away, a bolt of lightning crashed to earth from the oncoming tempest, followed by a peal of thunder that sounded ominous as an artillery barrage. This was a fast-moving storm, and a perceptibly violent one. Gusts of wind began whipping tumbleweeds about as darkness claimed the heavens.

"Stop the elephants and get in the coach," Omar yelled over the howling wind to Halim. The mahout needed no urging. He slid down the rope as if it were greased. The little man had not closed the door behind him when the first heavy drops of rain began splatting on the thirsty earth.

Barney scampered down from the observation deck followed by Omar, who quickly folded the ladder and closed the door with a slam.

"I must say," Halim said with a gasp, "this is shaping up to be a bugger of a storm. Texas is tough country, Boss."

"Generally they don't last long," Dallas said. "But they are exciting while they're going on."

A tremendous gust of wind shook the wagon, and a clap of thunder rattled the windows. A heavy pinging on the roof announced the arrival of hailstones; some of the icy white balls that could be seen bouncing off the ground were large as hen's eggs. There was a sharp clinking sound when a stone cracked one of the side windows.

"I do hope the elephants will be all right," Mabel said loudly.

"They've got tough hides," Omar replied over the roaring din. "I doubt the hail will do them any harm."

Halim turned to stare out the newly cracked window. The skinny mahout fidgeted with his turban. "Ain't the hail we need to worry about, Boss."

Barney's bearded face rose with the sudden realization of what Halim meant. Before he could say a word, a searing flash from a huge bolt of lightning striking the ground near the coach spoke his fears for him.

"That was close, too close," Omar said. "Lucky it didn't hit us."

"Boss, I got a bad feeling." Halim grabbed onto a door handle, then thought better of the idea and remained inside. Some of the hailstones hammering away at the circus wagon were now as big as a fist, and rain was coming down in torrential sheets. A person couldn't see past a few feet.

"I should never have come to Texas." Omar shook his bald head sadly. "I always thought Cleveland was the worst place on earth. Now I know I was seriously mistaken."

"Oh, this storm will be over right soon, an' nothing like it will happen again for a coon's age." Barney shrugged indifferently. "We're just suffering from bad timing is all."

Dallas said, "The thing to remember is that Poxon and Latts are having to endure the same storm. And they're not enjoying the benefits of a nice wagon to wait it out in."

"I do wish them to be miserable, but unhurt." Omar looked sadly at the little girl's body that was now wrapped in a blanket and tied securely to a seat. "My goal is to kill them as slowly and painfully as possible. When a man is hunting animals, the object is to make a clean kill. Those two are pure evil, worse than any living thing I've ever believed existed. They are beneath an animal."

"According to the teachings of Krishna, in the *Bhagavad-Gita*"—Halim continued to worry with his white turban—"all living things have a soul. But I do not think Krishna ever met these Poxon or Latts people."

"Any God worth his prayers should have struck them down long ago." Barney studied a stub of cigar, trying to decide if there was enough left to smoke, or if he should simply chew the remains. "Maybe, with all the lightning bolts flying about, he might finally be getting around to it."

"I intend to lend him as much help to that end as needed," Dallas said. "Tiberius Poxon went and hung an innocent and mighty pretty gal in my stead. I have a debt to pay that man no matter how long it takes."

Mabel shook her head sadly. "All of these horrible

killings." She looked at Dallas, tears welling in her blue eyes. "I would hate living here in the West."

"Ma'am," Dallas replied, "I can understand your feelings on the matter, considering all that's happened lately. But there are lots of good people and good towns in Texas. It's just that the outlaws and killers cause more focus to be put on 'em. Preachers have a hard time filling half the pews on a Sunday. Now a hanging draws one heck of a crowd."

Mabel Washburn was trying to figure out the bounty hunter's logic when, as suddenly as it had begun, the raging storm relinquished its hold on the land. Scant seconds later, a ray of sunlight shot though an opening in the clouds.

"I told y'all that storms don't hang around long in West Texas," Barney commented. "Once things dry out, no one'll notice it ever happened."

Halim's dusky face was a mask of tension when he unlatched the door and jumped out. The mahout gave a scream of anguish. "Oh, Boss!" he yelled. "Come see. We have terrible trouble, terrible, terrible."

Harry Latts shook a few drops of rain from his English-style Bollinger hat, then placed it back on his head, taking care to position it just so. "I must say, Mr. Poxon, that was quite some storm. We are fortunate to have found this ledge of rocks for shelter."

"Not all *that* lucky, Mr. Latts." Tiberius Poxon stared from the opening at his horse, which lay on the ground, whinnying piteously. The hapless animal was bleeding from numerous places where huge hailstones had opened long cuts. Others had slammed hard into the animal, beating it down. "Stupid thing shouldn't have bolted out into the open. There was simply no controlling it."

"Storms cause panic in horses quite often, sir. Nothing you could have done would have prevented its demise. But this did cause an unfortunate circumstance; now we will be forced to ride double."

Tiberius kept watching the horse as it pawed mindlessly at nothing. "Only until we come to the next way station, Mr. Latts. Then we can proceed as we have been. I am growing increasingly anxious to reach El Paso. The sooner I can begin to reclaim my town, the better. As the Good Book admonishes us in Galatians, 'Thrust in thy sickle, and reap: for the time is come for thee to reap: for the harvest of the earth is ripe.'"

Harry Latts wondered if his lunatic employer had ever heard the words about sowing a wind and reaping a whirlwind, or something like that. There seemed to be about any excuse in the Bible a crazy person needed to justify their actions. "Yes, sir," was all he thought safe to say. He knew all too well how unpredictable religious zealots could be.

Tiberius Poxon walked from beneath the sheltering ledge of rock that had saved them from the ravages of the hailstorm. He breathed deeply and looked about, studying the cactus-studded wasteland that seemingly had greened in mere moments. "'Small showers last long, but sudden storms are short,' the Bard so aptly wrote in *Richard the Second*. I find the brilliance of his observations to be stunning in their accuracy."

Latts wondered if possibly this Bard person might have written some of the Bible. He wasn't able to read any book, so he couldn't be sure on that point. It wouldn't be prudent to show ignorance on the matter, however. "Yes, sir, that Bard fellow certainly knew his stuff."

Poxon gave a sigh, pulled his pistol, and thought about

shooting his wounded horse behind the ear, killing it instantly. Then he shrugged and returned the gun to its holster. The animal deserved to suffer for causing him such inconvenience. "Help me remove the saddle and my bags, Mr. Latts. I will require these items later."

"The horse is going to be plenty loaded carrying the two of us. Perhaps it would be a good idea to leave the saddle. I'm rather certain it can be, ah, . . . replaced, at the next way station that should only be a few miles ahead."

"Of course, you are correct. A man of understanding hath wisdom."

Harry wondered who had penned that last crock, not that it mattered. Tiberius Poxon was becoming more unhinged by the moment. Now would be a grand time to simply shoot the lunatic, grab up the money, and ride off. Only some deep-seated splinter of loyalty kept him from doing just that. *Too much honesty is a terrible cross to bear.* Latts shook his head as if to toss the thought from his mind. He was becoming as loony as his employer. "I'll help you recover your property, sir."

"Thank you, Mr. Latts. Of course I shall require you to ride bareback. I really cannot suffer the indignity of riding into a stage station without being in a saddle. Even though the witnesses will never have any opportunity to tell others of the happening. I'm certain you are able to understand my predicament when it comes to keeping up appearances."

I'll be riding right behind him. A quick slice across his throat with my nice sharp knife would save a bullet. "Of course, sir." Harry Latts helped Poxon cut the money-laden saddlebags loose from the fallen horse. Moments later they were once again headed west, traveling slowly beneath a breaking blue sky.

Chapter 29

Barney Handley stood on muddy earth, his hands shoved deep into the pockets of his Levi's, chewing on a cigar stub while studying the still-smoking carcass of the dead elephant. It had obviously been done in by a bolt of lightning that had hit the hapless beast square in the forehead. At least the jagged black hole there made him believe that to be the case.

"Sure is a big fellow," Barney said. "An average tribe of Indians could live off all of this meat for a year most likely."

The others gathered about the crispy pachyderm gave the bearded old fellow a skewed look. Barney's strange remarks often caused people to quickly change the subject in hopes of derailing his train of thought.

"Poor Halim is brokenhearted," Mabel said, her sad eyes focused on the skinny mahout who, tears streaming down his dusky cheeks, was hugging the unharmed lead elephant's trunk.

Omar Lassiter spoke quickly to his wife. "I feel the same way myself. That was a thousand-dollar elephant." He lowered his head. "We never should have come to Texas; lightning is better behaved back East."

Dallas was studying their fix from a pragmatic viewpoint. "We're going to have our work cut out for us. I'm guessing we've got a couple of tons of dead elephant to get out of the way. Then, I wonder if the only one we've got left can pull that big circus wagon."

"Her name was Chitra," Halim said with a sob. "And she weighs almost as much as Boss's traveling home, at least four tons."

"This is a task to study on." Barney decided he had enough cigar left to be worth lighting. He fished a match from a shirt pocket. "A bucksaw would be useful."

"One thing's for certain," Omar said through pinched lips. "We're going to have to cut the harness running underneath her to free up the lead elephant. That's a shame; cost a lot that harness did."

"Naraka will grieve for a long time," Halim said, stroking the elephant's cheek. "They have been mated many years. But once we have cut the unfortunate Chitra loose, and made the harness ready, he will happily pull the wagon, though not so fast as before. Naraka understands we must proceed with all dispatch or other innocents shall surely die. He does not wish this to be, Boss."

"Reckon I never figured on a circus elephant having any feelings," Barney said, struggling to light his short cigar without burning himself. "There's a lot different animals than we're used to having in these parts."

"Where there is life, there is a spirit, a soul." Halim went to the coach and returned carrying a wicked-looking knife with an oddly curved blade. Every eye watched as the little man sliced away the harness from the dead elephant's body. "Help me find a rope to run from the wagon to Naraka. We must pull the boss's traveling home around poor Chitra, then make ready to continue our manhunt."

Halim then surprised the Handleys when he made a

small cut into the back of his hand, smeared a bit of blood on both sides of the blade before returning the odd knife to its curved sheath. He noticed their questioning expression. "This is a Gurkha knife. It is a soldier's weapon in my country, never to be taken from its case and returned without drawing blood."

"Why's that?" Dallas asked.

"It is a custom of the Hindu people."

"I'd reconsider painful tactics like that over here. Generally, though, I reckon the blood wouldn't necessarily be your own."

"Special circumstance here, Boss." The mahout turned to replace the Gurkha knife into the coach. "But you are correct, Boss. In India too, a person seldom needs to whack on their own selves to keep the custom alive. Bad folks are all over."

While Omar, Halim, and his father worked to push back, then rehook, the circus wagon, Dallas kept looking west along the twisting narrow band of road that glistened in the newborn sunlight like a wet snake. His brow lowered, then lined with concern. He had seen both stagecoaches and freighters alike mired up to their hubs in mud trying to cross draws after a deluge like the one they had just experienced. Being one elephant short was a worrisome situation. If Lassiter's heavy traveling home was to get stuck, they would be in trouble, serious trouble. He wondered why he had allowed the showman to talk them into leaving their horses behind. Omar claimed they didn't have the stamina to keep up and drank more water than could be spared. But Dallas was familiar with conducting a manhunt from horseback.

It would be a grievous occasion if Tiberius Poxon and Harry Latts made it to civilization, disappeared for an appropriate amount of time, then showed up back in Devil's Gate armed with a Philadelphia lawyer and literally got away with wholesale murder. The quicker those two met with a hot slug of lead, the better. Even more gratifying would be if the bullet came from his gun, sent with Velvet Dawn's regards. The bounty hunter gave an impatient snort, then went to help out his companions. Time was of the essence.

The task took longer than expected. Naraka, the elephant, refused for the longest while to allow himself to be harnessed, probing and testing his dead mate with his long truck. After a while the huge pachyderm backed away, raised his tusked head, and gave a loud, sad trumpet to the heavens. The plaintive cry was similar to the one Omar had made when he had held the little dead girl in his arms at the way station.

"Naraka has said his farewells to her soul," Halim said simply. "Now he is ready to go. There is nothing to hold him here now that the spirit has fled."

The mahout was eerily correct in his statement. After the mournful trumpeting, the huge elephant began acting anxious to be under way. He followed Halim's tender urging with the wand without hesitation.

After much improvising of the harness with rope and leather lacing, the mahout climbed on Naraka's gray back and lightly touched his forehead with the thin stick, starting the huge circus wagon lumbering slowly westward into a lowering sun.

Before they were out of sight, the sky behind them was a seething mass of circling black vultures.

"Well, now we know where those two murderers holed up for the storm." Dallas motioned to a deep depression in a cliff side with sheltering ledges of red sandstone jutting overhead for several feet. "Lucky bastards."

"They ain't *that* lucky." Barney had jumped from the

coach to point out a saddled horse lying on the ground down the slope a short distance. When the obviously battered animal raised its head to give a low wheezing grunt of agony, the old artilleryman said, "Those son's o' bitches. They didn't even have the decency to put that poor horse out of its misery."

Dallas walked around the elephant to the dying animal. Without hesitation, he pulled out his Colt and fired a shot into the horse's ear. The animal was so weak, it did not have the strength to even jerk back from the bullet, simply going limp.

"Things appear to be somewhat evening out," Omar Lassiter commented from his seat high on the wagon. "We have been slowed, but now it seems they are being forced to ride double."

"There's another stage stop maybe eight or so miles ahead," Dallas said. "After those two get there, and if they stay true to form, that won't be a problem for them."

Omar cocked his head; a serious expression grew to mask his normally cherubic face. "Boys, I fear our bounty hunter's prognostications may have already been realized."

Dallas gave a snort, then dashed to the observation deck to join Omar in staring at a distant thin column of black smoke twisting its way skyward in front of a dying sun.

"We'll be there before dark," Omar said to Halim. "Take us ahead with all possible speed."

"I hope no more dead, Boss, but I think these bad men have killed again."

"We'll get them," Dallas said firmly. "This is one manhunt that I'll not give up on even if we wind up having to chase those murderers down the main street of El Paso."

The elephant gave a brief trumpet. "Naraka agrees,

Boss." The mahout did not need to employ a touch
of his wand before the wagon began creaking west,
somewhat faster than before.

"The worst is not, so long as we can say, 'This is the
worst,' or so said the Bard." Tiberius Poxon kept his
position on the saddle, staring unbelievingly at the
burning way station.

"I'd venture Mr. Bard was correct when it comes to
this situation." Harry Latts jumped down from their
shared horse to study the man's body, lying in front of
an open corral gate, that had several arrows sticking
from out of his back.

"Apache," Harry said. "Likely a renegade band of
Geronimo's followers that didn't want to go live on a
reservation."

"Ironic, isn't it Mr. Latts." Tiberius spoke in a dron-
ing voice, as if he were reciting from a book. "We have
gone out of our way to make our raids appear to be the
work of the fierce Apache; now, it seems, the *real* Indians have appeared to cause us severe problems."

Harry Latts didn't have any idea what an iron had to
do with their fix. "From the looks of things, the Apache
have only been gone from here less than an hour. I
hope we do not run into them. From the number of
tracks, I think there may be over two dozen braves on
the rampage."

"Those heathen red devils stole all of the horses,"
Tiberius droned, stating the obvious.

"They did that, sir." Latts forced himself to calm
down. He walked over to the rock water tank beside a
still-pumping windmill. "At least we have water for us
and our only horse. Then we should be on our way. I

have a feeling in my bones we are being pursued. And that they are close now. Quite close."

Tiberius Poxon urged the horse toward the tank. "Look to see if you can find any coal oil, Mr. Latts. Then once we are finished with the water, we should toss that man's body in, along with any others that may be lying about. Denying succor to one's enemies is paramount."

Harry Latts turned away, a pained expression on his pockmarked face. *If I were not an honorable man, I would shoot you off that horse and head north.* Ignoring his thoughts, no matter how attractive they might be, the hired gun began to poke around the raided, burning way station looking for some means to poison the water.

Chapter 30

"I didn't think we'd make it through that last draw." Dallas stood leaning on the brass railing atop the mud splattered circus wagon. "I'd reckon elephants are a whole lot stronger animals than I'd thought. This thing must have bogged down a solid three feet."

"Naraka weighs more than our traveling home." Omar sat at his usual seat high on the front of the coach. He had a dead cigar clamped tight between his teeth as he stared intently at the smoking way station that was drawing near. "And yes, pound for pound, I believe they are the strongest animals on the face of the earth."

Dallas said sincerely, "I'm sorry about what happened to your other elephant. Being struck by lightning isn't an easy thing to predict out here where it seldom rains. I'd venture her being so big was what caused that bolt to hit where it did, especially if the elephant had its trunk struck up in the air at the time."

"Halim would say it was fate."

"No, it was a lightning strike," Barney said with finality, climbing up the ladder to the observation deck. "We close enough to see anything yet?"

"Will be in a few minutes, Dad." Dallas squinted into

a lowering sun where fiery red fingers were interspersed with black clouds as if the sun was trying to keep its grasp on the day. "Then we can see how many innocent folks got killed this time."

"Well, I'd say this is an interesting turn of the cards." Barney had bolted from the coach even before it creaked to a halt, rifle at the ready. He now stood near the smoking embers of the stage station looking down at a dead man with arrows sticking from out of his back.

"Considering the horses are plain missing instead of being shot where they stood, I would reckon you're right on that point, Dad." Dallas jumped to the drying earth and began walking around, eyeing the ground.

Omar stood up on his high seat to survey the area. "I only see the one body. Maybe our quarry has gotten lazy, as you mentioned earlier."

"You standing up there wearing that red jacket makes a mighty tempting target for anyone about with an itchy trigger finger," Barney said, sending the showman scurrying from his perch to join them.

"I wasn't thinking too clearly," Omar wheezed. "That wasn't smart of me at all."

"Well, you didn't get shot and you ain't got any arrows sticking out of your hide, so I reckon you proved the Apache have moved on. And most likely so have Poxon and Latts."

Omar Lassiter paled, a few beads of sweat popping out on his forehead. His dark eyes flashed wildly about the countryside. "Are there *real* wild Indians out here?"

Dallas nodded. "Real as a snakebite. They're likely some of Geronimo's band that didn't want to try out the climate in Florida. There's a lot of young bucks who want to cling to the old ways. But the Indians that did this are long gone."

Halim, who had been watching Dallas, came to him. "What does the ground tell you, Boss?"

"I'm studying tracks left behind by the men who struck this way station." Dallas motioned to the empty corral. "The rain softened the earth and the tracks are easy to read. First, there were well over a dozen Indians. Their horses are always unshod, so their tracks stand out like a boil on a whore's nose.

"The hoof marks over there are shod, which came from the horses they stole from the stage line. That's why we knew before that Indians weren't responsible for those other attacks; horses are like money to the Apache. Killing them would be like someone robbing a bank, then burning the loot. What I do notice that's mighty interesting is one lone mount that was shod came in from off the road, went over all the other tracks, and went toward that water tank yonder."

"I'm betting it was our lovelies, Poxon and Latts." Barney lowered an eyebrow. "The tracks settin' deep?"

"Yeah, Dad, they're riding double. That means both of 'em are still among the living, just slowed down a tad."

Barney strode to the rock water tank beside a squeaking windmill and peered into its depths. "We got ourselves another surprise. The water looks okay. At least there's no dead animals or coal oil floating in here."

Halim said, "I think these Apaches took everything worth stealing. Then I think they set fire to the rest. A meeting of two bad peoples. I think in this country they call this a 'pissing match.'"

"Close enough," Barney said with a thin grin. "It's just too bad Poxon an' Latts didn't show up here a mite earlier. Being caught by the Apache would be downright fitting for those two murderers."

"They would simply have killed them," Omar said with a disgusted shrug. "Frankly, I'd prefer worse."

Dallas motioned to the dead man. "Not really. That fellow was shot out of convenience. There were most likely other folks hereabouts. Kids and women are commodities to be used or traded, like horses. Men captives, on the other hand, are used for entertainment and tests of courage."

"Sometimes," Barney said after finally deciding to spit out his stub of cigar, "they'll take to skinnin' a man alive. The more skin you can stand to lose without screaming, the more impressed those Apache are with your bravery. I heard tell of a man in Arizona Territory they peeled away on for two days, skinnin' an arm, his face, an' one leg. Well, sir, that feller, a German if I recall correctly, never let out a peep. Them redskins were so impressed they let him go. Hear he owns a saloon in Tombstone these days. Good business he does too. Folks come in an' have a drink just to get a gander at him. By all accounts he's a memorable sight."

Halim clucked his tongue. "I was warned New York was a dangerous place. It really wasn't, but the West makes the waterfront of Calcutta seem tranquil by comparison."

"They bothered by the Apache over there too?" Barney asked.

"No, Boss." Halim turned to hide his grin. "But in India we have many just as bad." Then the little man scampered away to unhook the elephant so it could water and have a bath to wash away the mud that splattered its legs and underbelly.

"We'll rest here for a spell," Dallas said. "After we've had ourselves a meal and a smoke, the full moon will give us plenty of good light to travel by."

"Naraka will need some sleep," Omar said. "So will all of us."

"There's always plenty of time to sleep after a manhunt's over." Dallas reached into the showman's red jacket and extracted a couple of slim black cigars. "You can bet Tiberius Poxon and Harry Latts are not going to slow any; they're running for their very lives. Keep reminding yourself on that point. I can think of only one good thing that'd make me tarry longer than necessary."

"What's that?"

"The knowledge that they and that band of renegade Apache caught up with each other. By the tracks I saw leading away, they're all heading for the next way station."

Omar borrowed a line from Halim. "Oh, bugger," he said.

Chapter 31

"This is becoming an increasingly uncomfortable journey for me, Mr. Latts," Tiberius Poxon snorted in disgust, taking note of the rising full moon that was beginning to fill the desert with an eerie, wan light. "I do believe I am developing a blister due to your constantly trying to jam me into the saddle horn."

I can easily remove you from all pain. It would be my pleasure. Believe me on this. "Sorry, sir, but the saddlebags draped over my shoulders are quite heavy from the weight of all of your gold coins. And this horse is definitely a rough one to ride. I apologize for the inconvenience, but the way station cannot be much farther. I am certain that quite soon things will once again be coming our way."

"And makes us rather bear those ills we have than to fly to others we know not of?"

Harry Latts shut his eyes and took a long deep breath before answering. "More wisdom from Mr. Bard's pen, sir?"

"Ah, my dear Latts. When we are once again in Devil's Gate, as is my just destiny, and my mansion is repaired, I shall instruct you in the classics. There are many, many wonderful and comforting passages in the tomes of Shakespeare. As a partial reward for your fealty, I will make you a gift of his works—a leather-bound set no less."

I like the idea of a tome. Putting you inside of one, that is. Harry Latts was barely capable of signing his name, his skills running more toward the pragmatic placement of bullets into other people. He felt that his increasingly loony employer had paid him some form of a compliment, however. It would just be nice if he phrased his words in nice, plain, simple English, without quoting some overeducated dead guy. "Thank you, sir. I appreciate that. I believe that I also would enjoy reading a book by Mr. Bard too."   •

Tiberius Poxon gave a sincere chuckle. "Ah, my dear Mr. Latts, so you shall, once I have reclaimed my domain. As we travel together across this sea of troubles and travails, I value your loyalty all the more. Your rewards will be great indeed. Trust me."

Harry shifted the money-laden saddlebags to another position. He really hated to hear Poxon compliment him on being loyal, then go on to say he actually *trusted* him. That chafed worse than those leather saddlebags against his neck. When people acted up, doing them in was usually quite enjoyable. Placing an employer in his grave when he trusted you was a bird of a totally different feather. Killing a man under these conditions could cause nightmares later. Or not. Harry decided he needed to think some more on the matter. "Oh, I do trust you, sir." *For the moment anyway.*

Tiberius Poxon stiffened and reined the horse to a stop.

"You see something." Harry Latts said; his voice grew low and trailed off into silence. With the bright Apache killing moon now full in the sky, it wasn't difficult at all to make out the large group of Indians mounted on horseback that were lined up along the top of a low ridge, possibly a half mile away. It was also plain to see that they were all facing Poxon and Latts.

"We have ourselves a conundrum, Mr. Latts. Behind us, I fear, are those wishing me ill. Ahead lies our future, our fortunes, and our destiny. Now there has arisen yet another obstacle to plague us. I fail to recall any words of the Bard that might give us courage and direction."

"How about 'We're in deep shit'? That oughtta cover the situation."

"Crass, but accurate, Mr. Latts. I fear that two men on one horse cannot hope to outrun those savages."

I was thinking the same thing. "Yes, sir," was all he could come up with to say while trying to decide whether to use his knife or gun to remove the excess baggage from in front of him.

"Well, well, Mr. Latts, our fortunes seem to have changed in a matter of moments." Poxon pointed a finger at a stagecoach coming from the west. "I doubt those red devils will care to go against both our guns and those that are surely on yon stage."

Harry Latts released his grip on the hilt of his razor-sharp bowie knife. Tiberius might be a loony, but he was correct in his assessment of the Apache. The Indians quickly turned and rode off toward the distant, dark mountains to the south.

"I believe it will be safe for us to approach the stage without concern," Poxon said. "The telegraph lines are all along the railroad, which is many miles to the north. I doubt they have heard any news of, ah, any *incidents* to cause them undue alarm."

Latts chuckled. "With the night being so light, I'm sure the driver and the guard must have took notice of all those Indians. Them being about will serve to make what we did at those other way stations look like the work of the Apache. Luck does seem to be turning to our side."

Poxon spurred the horse onward to meet the stagecoach. "After we've made our acquaintances and we see who all is there to contend with, I'll shoot the guard, then the driver. With your skilled use of a pistol, I'm certain you can take care of the passengers."

"The element of surprise is always an effective tactic, sir. Very few people expect a friendly, smiling man to whip out a gun and start shooting them without some warning."

"I agree. Let's go get acquainted with our newfound friends and benefactors."

Halim signaled the elephant to stop, then slithered down the rope to inspect the bodies lying alongside the road. In the yellow bright moonlight, the splotches of blood on their clothing glistened like black oil. "Oh, Boss," the mahout yelled, "there are five dead here; three of them are women."

Barney and Dallas were by Halim's side in a brief moment, followed by a panting Omar Lassiter. There was obviously no need to check for signs of life. Each person had been shot square in the heart.

"Saloon girls," Barney said. "Pretty ones too. I can't figure why anyone would harm a woman."

Dallas said, "What I am wondering is how they came to be out here. I don't see any horses, and I don't think the Apache had any hand in this. A few of those Indians likely have rifles, but the feller they killed at the way station was shot full of arrows. I'm betting . . ."

"What does the ground tell you, Boss?" Halim asked as Dallas walked around inspecting tracks by wan light.

"Poxon and Latts aren't burdened with riding

double anymore. There are tracks where what was most likely a stagecoach turned around here."

Barney snorted. "They probably just rode up to that stage, acting all friendlylike. Then once they sized up the situation, they killed these innocent folks in cold blood."

"None of these girls are over twenty," Omar said, removing his bowler and holding it to his chest. "They were no threat to anyone. Why did they kill them like this?"

"No witnesses," Dallas said bluntly, glaring off to the west. "There's not one person left alive to tell who did all of these murders. That's what Poxon and Latts are counting on to keep from being hung."

"And now they're gotten themselves a stagecoach," Omar said through clenched teeth. "I feel badly saying this, but we really should not spare the time to cover these poor unfortunates from predators or coyotes. We are close to those bastards, very close. I can feel it in my bones."

Barney bent down and touched a finger to the chest of one of the dead men. "This blood's mighty fresh. I'm betting they got shot no more than three or four hours ago." He looked at Omar. "I agree with both your bones and your plan to stay on their heels. If we can't catch up with 'em and settle their hash right shortly, there'll be other folks in need of burying."

Halim shook his head sadly. "Their spirits have fled to the next world. I hope them happiness there. To be struck down for trusting another is a terrible thing, Boss. A very terrible thing."

"You're right, Halim," Dallas said, turning to the circus wagon. "Let's go get those son's o' bitches."

"Boss," Halim said running to climb on the elephant. "I will urge Naraka to pull faster."

When the huge coach lumbered by the murdered victims that lay on the now-dry desert, bathed in wan light from an Apache moon, everyone mouthed a silent vow of vengeance. A vow they hoped to be able to keep before any more innocent souls were murdered simply to cover up two killers' trail.

Chapter 32

Bertha Botts downed a healthy shot of Old Pepper. As the soothing amber fluid began to calm the nagging pain in her back, she studied first her cards, then the expression on her husband's face. The old geezer had been needing a shave for all the thirty years they had been married. And Ira never had learned not to let his eyes betray him whenever he held a losing hand.

They were both getting too old to run a stage stop in the barren reaches of West Texas, yet neither would ever admit the fact. The bales of hay and sacks of grain were heavier to tote these days. And the horses harder to catch and harness when a stagecoach passed through. Yet the fifty dollars the Overland company paid them every month, along with a place to live, was more than they would have earned in a nice town, like San Angelo, where their two grown sons lived.

"I'll raise you a nickel," Ira Botts said.

"You must be holding better than I think you are." Bertha eyed the whiskey bottle. It had been full when she had uncorked it at noon. Now only a few meager sips remained in the bottom. Her back still hurt, however. She divided the dregs between their two glasses and tossed the bottle out the open window, where it crashed onto a pile nearly as high as the sill. There was a full case to open and another shipment due next week. Suffering needlessly wasn't in Bertha Bott's cards.

"I'll just see your nickel, you old poop," Bertha said seriously. "And I'm raising you another nickel."

Ira fidgeted with his cards. "I ain't got another nickel, Ma. You've done cleaned my clock again. I swan, woman, I'd believe you were cheatin' on me except for the fact that I know you ain't smart enough to pull any wool over my eyes."

"If you don't let me trim that mop settin' on your head, that wool will fall there without any of my doing." She chugged her puny amount of whiskey. "If'n you can't raise, the pot's mine, y'old coot."

"I swear you're up to . . ." His voice trailed off at the sound of an approaching stagecoach from the east.

"Ma," Ira said with a cock of his head. "There ain't no stage due through here till late tomorrow afternoon. Joe and Darryl packin' those purty li'l saloon gals was supposed to be the last one."

"Now I remember why you're losing. You likely singed your peepers gawkin' at those girls."

"Ain't no harm in lookin', Ma. An' them wimmin weren't dressed like they were to be ignored. The company expects us to treat the passengers good, an' I aim to please."

"Yeah, well, I'm gonna meet whoever's coming with a scattergun. Might be Apache."

"Drivin' a *stagecoach.* Bertha, I wonder about you at times. Most of the time actually."

As the stagecoach creaked to a stop in front of the lonely way station, the bright killing moon hanging high in a satin-black sky allowed the old couple who came outside to plainly see it was the stage that had passed through earlier. And they did not recognize either of the two men sitting on the driver's seat.

Bertha cocked the hammers on a double-barreled twelve-gauge shotgun and pointed it square at the strangers. Her husband came out carrying an old Navy pistol.

"Where's Joe an' Darryl?" Bertha said firmly. "And why'd y'all come back here for anyways?"

Tiberius Poxon stared into the twin dark maws of the shotgun wondering if he or Latts might be fast enough to dispatch the old bat before she could pull the triggers. That scenario seemed most unlikely. Taking another approach seemed healthier.

"Glad to see you are armed, ma'am." Poxon forced alarm into his voice. From the corner of his eye he noted Harry Latts's hand resting on the butt of his Colt. "It's Indians. They hit the stage. We're freighters who came along at just about the same time. Those two men you asked about are in the coach. I'm afraid they are badly wounded and in need of attention."

The shotgun stayed pointed at them, only now it was joined by Ira's .36 Navy revolver.

"Where's them purty gals at?" Ira yelled.

"Apache got 'em," Harry Latts answered.

"There's lot of bad men about," Bertha hollered. "You two keep your hands where I can see 'em. Stand up nice an' slowlike and drop those gun belts. Then we'll take a gander inside that stage."

"Those men are bad hurt." Poxon's voice was showing fear. "You're wasting time."

"You'll join 'em if'n you don't do what I'm tellin' you to do," Bertha growled.

Harry Latts had been in enough tight situations before not to expect a miracle. His loony boss wasn't going to talk the old bat with a shotgun into lowering

her aim. It was a long shot, but he flipped out his pistol
as he bolted low toward the front of the stage.

"Jaysus H. Hillbilly Christ!" Tiberius Poxon screamed
as twin loads of shotgun pellets were blasted their way.
Harry Latts's hat flew off into the darkness and he
dropped flat on the seat beside him. Poxon didn't need
to coax the horses. The blast from the gun sent them
into a panic, knocking him back onto the top of the
stagecoach when it bolted forward.

"Well shoot at 'em, you old coot!" Bertha yelled at
her husband. "What are you waitin' for?"

"Ain't got but the five shells, Ma. Be a shame to need
'em later an' not have 'em. Besides, I think the message
you sent 'em most likely took. Reckon the law'll handle
those two."

"Wonder what happened to the folks on that stage."

"Ma," Ira said, "I don't want to think about it."

"I swan." Ira Botts added a healthy jolt of Old
Pepper to his morning cup of coffee. "I reckon I can
finally tell folks that I've seen the elephant."

"That's a fact," Barney Handley said from across the
dining room table inside of the way station. "Sure the
only one I ever set eyes on too."

"It was good to have you an' Dallas show up." Bertha
poked firewood into the huge Majestic kitchen range.
"We ain't seen y'all for a coon's age. If you can spare the
time, I'll fry up a mess of bacon an' buckwheat pancakes. Would've had eggs to go with it, if'n Ira hadn't
forgot he set the only dozen we owned in his chair,
then plopped down on 'em. I worry about that man."

"You think you might've shot the small fellow?" Dallas
asked, eyeing the side of bacon. "He's a murderer by the
name of Harry Latts."

Bertha chuckled. "I can honestly say I gave him my best shot."

"He dropped, that's all we can say for certain." Ira smiled upon his coffee. "You see much of our boys up in San Angelo these days?"

Barney said, "Robert's one of my best customers in the saloon. Now Jim, well, him working as an undertaker, I suppose at my age I can be forgiven for not seekin' him out."

"Jim's the last one on earth to let you down." Bertha gave a hearty chuckle before turning serious. "Sorry to hear those two thugs who came through here a few hours ago went and killed those poor gals."

"There is a body in my traveling home," Omar Lassiter said gravely, "of a little girl they killed. I believe her to be no more than eight or nine years old." He sighed and added, "The poor thing was savaged before her neck was broken."

"If I'd known that, I'd have plugged 'em," Ira said. "Hard to tell what's in a man's heart just by lookin' at 'em."

"Reckon Dallas will settle with 'em, Pa." Bertha took a knife to the bacon and began placing thick slices into a deep cast-iron skillet. "He's been puttin' folks in the ground that desperately need it for a lot of years. I'm figurin' those two scallywags are on borrowed time. Heck, I may have pretty well perforated their hides already. Kinda hard to tell sometimes, especially at night."

"Kinda hard for you to tell in daylight," Ira said. He grinned at Barney. "Ma likes her toddies." Then he added another finger of Old Pepper to his coffee.

Mabel Washburn came inside. "Halim has watered the elephant. He says we can get under way any time now. He believes with them driving a stagecoach, we can overtake them in a few hours."

"I'd reckon it was somewheres past midnight when

Ma shot at 'em." Ira gave a motion with his head to an oak clock on the mantel behind the heating stove. "I need to get that thing fixed someday. Ain't worked since Grant was President."

"Neither have you, you old poop." Bertha stirred the sizzling bacon. "Breakfast will be ready in a shake."

"We shouldn't tarry," Dallas said, his voice low and faltering.

"Ah"—Barney shrugged—"we can kill 'em on a full stomach, sonny boy. Like Bertha said, they're already dead. The fact just ain't caught up with 'em yet."

"And we are getting no closer sitting here," Omar said. "But I do believe a brief repast to be in order. This manhunt has become most grueling."

"We've got lots of good mesquite honey to go with the flapjacks," Bertha said, flipping the bacon.

"I'll go fetch Halim," Mabel said. Ira nearly spilled his coffee when she stood.

Dallas looked at the old couple. "I'm really glad you two were on your guard."

Bertha shrugged. "Been out here too long not to. The law don't care much if you shoot someone, so I fail to see why Ira an' me need to hold off on the ammo."

"Ma an' me's got another case of both whiskey an' scattergun shells coming." Ira took a healthy drink of coffee. "If more folks were well prepared as us, Dallas my friend, you'd be forced to find other employment."

Dallas thought back on the five bodies only a few miles east. "Honestly, Ira, I'd gladly do that."

Bertha began mixing a big bowl of buckwheat pancakes. The sooner the manhunt resumed, the better.

Chapter 33

"I'm dying," Harry Latts groaned, holding a bloody hand clasped to the side of his head as he teetered from side to side on the seat of the stagecoach. "I can't believe that woman up and shooting me like she did. You just can't trust anybody these days."

"You sure are doing a lot of complaining for a man about to die." Tiberius Poxon turned to see how far they were from the way station. He couldn't see any lights, but it felt safer to continue on a few more miles. He was simply glad to have survived the encounter. "We'll stop when it's safe and see to your wounds."

"I ain't never been shot before." Latts gave a whine when he took his hand from his bleeding head and saw blackish droplets of fresh blood dripping onto the plank floor in front of the driver's seat. "Oh, God, I'm dying. I know I am. It hurts so *bad*."

Tiberius shook his head, mostly in anger. His employee had failed him. Latts was supposed to have shot both that man and woman before they could pull a trigger. It galled the mining magnate to have been let down at such a crucial moment. Some of those shotgun pellets had sung their way past him by mere inches. Poxon took a deep breath and exhaled slowly. He needed to calm down. After all, Harry Latts was the one bleeding, not him.

Better now, Tiberius Poxon began assessing his situation with a clear head. *Any* employee was always expendable, yet he realized his need for the services of Harry Latts had not ended. There were endless possibilities. The wounded gunman could be dropped alongside the road, hopefully behind some big rocks, to dispatch the men he knew were on his trail. That was how *truly* loyal employees should behave. Then, it struck him that maybe Latts's injuries were not immediately life-threatening. The man had, after all, been rather helpful to have along. At least he had until rather badly misjudging the woman at that last stage stop.

"I think it might be safe to stop here for a few moments." Poxon reined the six horses pulling the Concord to a halt. He had no real experience with gunshot wounds, but plugging any holes leaking blood would be a good place to start.

When the stage groaned to a stop and Tiberius had set and locked the brake, Harry Latts remained ominously quiet. Poxon had heard stories of men dying in a sitting position. There wasn't a lot of time to tarry, so he turned to his stricken employee and forcibly yanked the bloody hand from the man's head.

"Take it easy," Latts sobbed, proving he was still among the living. "I'm bleeding to death out of my ear."

"We have a good light out, but I'll fire up a match and take a close gander. There sure is a lot of blood, however."

Latts gave a low moan as Tiberius Poxon took three tries to fire the match. He leaned to one side and waited for his employer to tell him that his wound was a mortal one. *Any* wound hurting and bleeding as bad as this one simply *had* to be fatal.

"Umm," Poxon mumbled.

"Tell me the truth, sir. I can take it."

"I doubt that statement, Mr. Latts. I really do."

"How long do I have?"

"That's hard to say. If no one else shoots you, maybe thirty, forty years."

"What?" Harry Latts knew his boss was simply attempting to be kind to him in his last moments on earth.

"One of those shotgun pellets just took a small notch out the edge of your ear. Those type of wounds do bleed a lot, but you're barely hurt, Mr. Latts. Now buck up."

"Can you bandage it, you know, to stop all that blood loss?"

"I'd have to wrap it all the way around your head."

"Please, sir."

Tiberius Poxon gave a sigh. He had in the past run across men who were tough hard cases, impervious to any pain but their own. It was a surprising tendency to find in a hired gunfighter, however. Getting to El Paso quickly was the paramount goal. If stopping a minor wound from dripping blood was all it took to bring an end to his employee's hysterical whining and start them on their way again, so be it. There were several trunks on the stage. In the very first one, he found a nice shirt. He ripped a long piece from it, and in a few moments had wrapped it beneath Harry Latts's chin and tied it firmly at the top of his head.

"Are you sure I've only got shot through my ear?"

"Just a little piece missing out of the edge. You'll be fine. There hasn't been enough blood lost to fill a saucer." Poxon's voice turned firm. "Now that we know you are only slightly injured, Mr. Latts, I am going to start the stage for El Paso once again. Your job is to stay alert for danger on all fronts, especially our back trail. Our very survival is hinging on you."

"Yes, sir." Latts gave a sniff, then sat upright on the driver's seat. "You can depend on me."

Tiberius Poxon lowered his head to gain composure. A moment later he released the brake and started the stagecoach on its way west. A bright glow building on the jagged horizon behind them announced the birth of a new day.

Chapter 34

Omar Lassiter stood atop the observation deck of his lumbering circus wagon, joining Barney and Dallas Handley in leaning on the brass railing where they were keeping their eyes peeled for any sign of their quarry. There really was no reason to stay on the driver's seat and keep up any image out here. Halim always controlled the elephants, or sadly, as the case was now, the elephant.

"I'm surprised," Omar said, "there is not a lot more traffic along this road. I thought we would encounter numerous stagecoaches and freight wagons, but this is the loneliest stretch of road I have ever been on."

"The time was," Barney said keeping his gaze to the west, "you'd have been right about this being a busy road. But times are changing."

Dallas continued his father's conversation. "When the railroad came through to the north of here, that took over most of the freight and passengers. The Overland company only runs five, maybe six stages through here a week. Wasn't so long ago they ran that many every day."

Barney sighed. "It likely won't be too much longer

until they'll shut down all the way stations across West Texas. Those newfangled steam trains run cheaper an' are one helluva bunch faster. Load 'em up with coal and lots of water, they'll make it maybe three hundred miles in a day, even with stopping for freight, mail, an' people. Ain't no way a stagecoach can compete with speed like that."

Omar flashed a glance to their rear. "What will become of the folks like the Botts who've been out here for a lot of years?"

"Politicians," Dallas said, "call it the wheels of progress. They never bother to add that sometimes those wheels run over some mighty good people."

"I would truly hate to see those folks put out of work," Omar said. "But this world does seem to have started spinning faster than we are going to be able to keep up with. In Cleveland they even have electric cars to run along the streets these days."

"That would be an improvement over stepping around horse apples," Barney observed. "Sounds like a fine idea to me. And not having to put a saddle on the thing every time you wanted to go somewhere is a plus."

Omar began to mutter something about Cleveland, then decided to change the subject. The thought of that old couple they had left behind at the way station being out of a job depressed him. Or possibly it was remembering being in Cleveland that had put him into a funk.

"At least now I can understand why Tiberius Poxon and Harry Latts chose to travel this route." Omar took three long black cigars from his jacket, bit the end off one and stuck it into his mouth, then passed out the other two. "There are so few people out here, they stand a darn good chance of killing every witness to them even passing through these parts."

"That's a fact," Dallas said. "If they'd gone north and

hailed a train, that would have caused them to buy tickets, leaving a record and a lot of folks remembering seeing them. Heading out this way like they done gives 'em a chance to plumb disappear."

Omar cocked his head at a distant circling of buzzards. "What about that gal who got hung in Devil's Gate. Won't the law go after Poxon for that?"

Dallas shrugged. "I doubt it. The sheriff, Sinker Wilson, was the one who did the hanging. Any investigation into the matter, I'm betting, won't lead to any evidence that Tiberius Poxon had any hand in the matter." The bounty hunter gave a thin, satisfied grin. "But the last time I saw Sinker Wilson, he was in three pieces after I shot him in the middle with a cannon."

The circus owner decided he really did not want to know any more. People in the West had a much different outlook than they did in other places, or even other countries, for that matter. But there were the possible exceptions of France, or Morocco. He nodded at the horizon. "I wonder what those vultures have found to attract them."

"We'll find out when we get there," Barney said. "Might take us a half hour or more. Distance is deceiving out here in the desert."

"I've noticed that." Omar turned to the open staircase. "I should go down and see how my wife is doing. Having that body in the coach seems to have set Mabel's nerves on edge."

Barney shrugged. "Women do tend to be finicky about things like that."

Omar gave one last glace to the west, then went below to spend some time comforting his wife.

Dallas Handley waited until the huge wagon had groaned to a complete stop before releasing his grip on the brass rail to stand straight. "We were talking earlier about the wheels of progress running over people. I reckon we plumb overlooked wildlife."

Mabel had joined her husband on the observation deck to look at the sad sight of a buck deer that had gotten its leg snagged in a barbed-wire fence and died a slow, agonizing death.

"Leastwise it wasn't more human victims of Poxon and Latts," Barney said.

"This is terrible," Mabel sobbed. "Why would anyone build a fence out in the middle of nowhere in the first place?"

"There's a land baron out here in West Texas by the name of Ajax Wolfgang," Dallas said. "I heard tell he's trying to fence in every acre he owns. And I reckon he's not alone in doing that."

"Not too many years ago," Barney said, "this was open range. Herds of cattle were driven through here all the way to Dodge City, Abilene, or Pueblo, Colorado. In all that distance there wasn't a single strand of barbed wire to be found. Nowadays, even a deer can't walk around without coming to get snagged. I reckon I don't care for that. Not a bit."

Dallas continued on the subject of the land baron. "Ajax is dead set to mark out his territory. Last I heard he's got over a hundred square miles fenced. Then he'll either buy or acquire some more sections. People say he's got over twenty men working for him full time that do nothing but build more fences."

"Progress has its price," Omar said.

"Reckon everything comes with a price," Barney said. "But it's a terrible shame when you don't have a choice about paying it."

"Those men on that stagecoach are still keeping ahead of us." Dallas pointed to fresh wagon tracks in the road. "We'll run those horses of theirs to ground soon. Far as I know there's only one thing they could do that might cause them to get away from us."

"Yeah, sonny boy." Barney had a firm set to his jaw. "An' with us having no horses to go after 'em on, they might just get the job done."

"What are you getting at?" Omar asked with concern. "I believe it to be only a matter of time until we catch up with those murderers."

Mabel said, "They can't get away from us. Not after all of the people they've killed, including that poor little girl we have downstairs."

Dallas motioned to Halim to start the wagon moving again. "We can always hope they don't get to thinking."

"What's he getting at?" Omar repeated, looking straight at Barney.

"Those two have six horses that are pulling that stage-coach. If'n Poxon and Latts get either spooked or smart, they'll probably shoot four of those horses, keep-ing the best two. Then they'll saddle those, if they've still got saddles, or ride bareback and head off."

"We'll still overtake them," Omar said firmly.

"Not if they decide to ride off cross-country we won't," Dallas snorted. "We won't stand a chance if they do that. Our only hope is that they stay on the road and let us run 'em down."

Omar Lassiter said, "Let us cross that bridge when we come to it."

Moments after the huge traveling home had moved on, the multitude of circling turkey vultures began re-turning to feast on the remains of the hapless deer that had gotten caught and died in a needless barbed-wire fence.

Chapter 35

"Well, Mr. Latts," Tiberius Poxon said, speaking loudly to be heard over the ever-increasing squawking of a wheel badly in need of grease. "It appears that we are being subjected to the slings and arrows of outrageous fortune."

Harry Latts adjusted the bandage over his ear. "Is that another bit of wisdom from Mr. Bard's pen, sir?"

"Very perceptive. As a matter of fact it comes from *Hamlet*."

"This Hamlet fellow, did he have an axle burn out on his coach too?"

Poxon took a moment to compose himself before answering the idiotic gunman who couldn't bear the slightest pain. "You could say that he suffered some rather substantial misfortunes, as are we. Only I do hope our outcome will be an improvement over Hamlet's."

"Didn't he have some trouble with the Texas Rangers or some lawman up in Dallas? I've heard . . ."

Tiberius grabbed hold of the seat as the stagecoach gave a loud pop, followed by the rear of the coach thudding down and dropping onto the rocky ground. The mining magnate turned to see a smoking wheel roll past to smash into a clump of prickly pear cactus, spin around, and overturn.

Harry Latts had either jumped or been tossed to the ground. Tiberius Poxon climbed down to join him.

"I didn't expect to lose the whole damn wheel just because it started squeaking a little." Tiberius Poxon's face grew red with anger. "The Overland Stage Company is owned by a bunch of cheapskates who do not properly maintain their vehicles. I think the whole lot should be fired for incompetence."

"It certainly caused us to be between the devil and the deep blue sea." Harry Latts beamed at his competence in remembering this passage. He could not recall where he had heard it, but the quote sure covered their predicament. "Did the Bard say that?"

Poxon surveyed the burnt axle sticking inches deep into the roadway. He briefly wished his hired gunman was underneath the wreckage, then took a deep breath. "No, Mr. Latts, if I recall correctly it was not Shakespeare, but the wisdom is worthy of his pen. I fear that now, with our train conveyance disabled, we must study upon the perplexity of our situation."

Harry Latts looked at the distant wheel that was sending up a slender column of smoke. "A wheel come off our stagecoach."

"Yes, Mr. Latts, your percipience is quite commendable. I also have taken note of that fact. What we need to do is decide how best to repair the vehicle."

"We've got six horses. They're about tuckered out from being pushed like we've done, but we could cut 'em loose from the stage and ride them to El Paso."

Tiberious Poxon was taken aback by the gunslinger's pragmatic statement. For some odd reason, he had only thought of repairing the stagecoach. *I'm getting tired is all. Once I'm on a train heading out of El Paso for anyplace, I'm going to bathe, enjoy a bottle of good wine along with an excellent meal of oysters and steak, then climb into a nice comfortable berth and sleep for a full day and night.*

"An excellent suggestion," Tiberius said with obvious sincerity. "I do wonder how far we are from El Paso. The sooner we can catch a train the better."

"The last way station we burned, I saw a map of the stage routes on the wall. I studied it a bit before throwing coal oil on it and lighting a match. That thing was made from some kind of linen stuff. Sure caught fire easy."

"And the information on that map was?"

Harry Latts cocked his head in thought. "Well, sir. That station was before I got my ear shot by that mean woman. I'm reckoning we're gone over twenty miles from there. . . ."

"How far are we from El Paso, Mr. Latts? That is the question before us, and our goal."

"I'm trying to cipher here, sir. If I recall, that map showed the station—the last we set on fire—to be one hundred and twenty-five miles west of El Paso."

"I do believe you mean *east* of El Paso."

"Yeah." Latts lowered his brow in thought. "Guess I made a little mistake. I ain't really good with maps. But if we've made twenty miles since I got shot, all I gotta do is cipher how many miles it was between those two way stations, and subtract it from a hundred twenty-five. Then I'll have a fair-to-middling idea how to answer your question, sir."

"To keep from straining your intellect even more, let us assume the distance was twenty-five miles, which is, I believe, the average between way stations. That would lead one to assume we are approximately only a mere eighty miles or so from our goal."

"Those ciphers makes me assume the same thing."

"If we don't care about running those stupid horses to death, I believe we can make it in one long hard run."

"I suggest, sir"—Harry Latts gingerly touched his wounded ear to see if it was bleeding again; it cheered him to find it wasn't—"that we each choose a spare horse to lead, saddle only the best-looking two, then kill the extras."

"No, Harry, I don't think so." His use of such a familiar term to an employee surprised him. This had to be another manifestation of his utter fatigue. "We'll simply ride away with the four horses we choose and leave the others to go free. Perhaps the Apache will be blamed if we do this."

"Yeah." Harry Latts nodded in agreement. "I'm in hopes those dirty, bloodthirsty redskins will get blamed for all those people we were forced to, ah, *remove* from our pathway. Most folks in these parts won't take a lot of convincing. Your idea of turning loose those two horses is an excellent one, sir."

Tiberius pulled his gaze from the still-smoking stage-coach wheel to study the horizon. The country ahead of them was not jagged nor mountainous. It appeared that only rolling, cactus-studded hills stood between them and the much-needed comforts of a steam train heading anywhere. The crucial question in his mind was, when would be the best time to dispatch his milk-sop of a hired gunman? It wouldn't do to have Latts live to enter El Paso with him. Wouldn't do at all.

Harry Latts was the sole living witness to all of what they had been forced to do since leaving Devil's Gate. Of course he had to die. People, *all* people, were disposable, no matter how helpful they had been in the past. Besides, first-class travel by train was expensive. *Very* expensive. It would be far more economical to simply hire another gunman. Perhaps his next employee might be cast of sterner material and not panic at the sight of his own blood. There never seemed to be any shortage of young men anxious to prove their proficiency with a gun. Replacing Harry would present no difficulty. None at all. Briefly, he wished for a nice sharp ice pick, to make Latts's death appear to be an accident. Then, he reminded himself the Apache were about. Simply shooting the man a couple of times was all that it would take to shift the blame. *Always* shift the blame. That was what it took to get ahead in this world; look after yourself. And damn all others.

One more day, Poxon thought, *when I'm in sight of El Paso is when I'll shoot him. No use risking not getting my money's worth out of him first.*

"I'll go and start cutting the traces," Harry Latts said. "Then, I shall be happy to place your saddle on the best-looking of the lot. Riding bareback is most uncomfortable, but my saddle was unfortunately lost because of that awful hailstorm."

Tiberius smiled broadly. "Your reward will soon be forthcoming, Mr. Latts. I do *so* want you to know that I appreciate your fealty and intend to compensate you most liberally. But for now, as the Bard so aptly advised in *Venus and Adonis,* 'Make use of time, let not advantage slip.'"

"Yes, sir," Harry Latts said, taking out his razor sharp bowie knife and turning to the horses. "That Bard fellow sure knew his stuff."

A short while later, the two men, each leading a horse burdened with canteens of water and provisions, started off along the road to El Paso. They were both miffed by the fact that the stagecoach had not lost its wheel on some portion of the road where it would block any oncoming traffic. But they were once again on their way west, growing closer to destiny's door with each passing moment.

Tiberius Poxon did not notice Harry Latts's occasional loving glance at the heavy brown leather saddlebags draped across the back of his horse.

Chapter 36

"It looks like our lovelies have suffered another set-back," Barney Handley said as he peered inside the disabled stagecoach. "Too bad the thing didn't turn all the way over an' squash 'em like cockroaches."

"That would be too easy an end for those two murderers," Omar Lassiter said, wheezing his way to inspect the cut harness and traces. "I want them to pay for all the savagery they have done. And the more suffering tossed in, the better."

Dallas Handley took a puff on his cigar, studying the two horses that were standing a few feet away, nosing about for a bite of stunted grass. "I understand your feelings, Omar, but I've been dealing with evil men like Tiberius Poxon and Harry Latts for a lot of years. Take my advice and stop the hate. Look on 'em like rabid animals that have caused good people to die. The first thing is to stop the killings, no matter what. If a quick bullet between the eyes gets the job done, take the results with gratitude."

"I know," Omar sighed, "you are correct. It just seems fair to extract some retribution for that pitiful little girl they savaged and killed on her birthday along with all the other innocents. In the Bible, I think in the Book of Hosea, it says: 'They have sown the wind, and they shall reap the whirlwind.'"

Barney decided there wasn't anything of interest inside the stagecoach. He pulled his head out of the open door and turned to Omar. "That same Good Book also has a passage about God claiming vengeance is up to him, or something like that."

"Close enough." The circus owner shuffled his polished black boots in the powder-dry dirt. "You've got me convinced to be satisfied with simply killing them."

"There you go," Dallas said, walking ahead to inspect the road for tracks.

Halim had filled a large wooden bucket with water from a tank built into the circus wagon. After setting it in front of Naraka so the elephant could drink, the swarthy mahout scurried to the bounty hunter's side. The reading of tracks fascinated him.

"The ground talks to you once again," Halim said to Dallas.

"Yeah, come alongside me and you'll see. Now here you can see the tracks of four horses, one behind the other, which means they're each leading a packhorse. More than likely they'll be making a hard push for El Paso, carrying along all the water and grain for the horses they can. I figure we're only about a day and a half away from that city if a person doesn't care to risk killing their horse. And I reckon we all know how much concern Poxon and Latts are prone to display."

"They are bad men, Boss. The worst kind."

"On the good side, they're heading straight down the road like good boys. Makes chasing them down a lot easier when you don't have to take the time to follow their tracks across country."

Halim walked up to atop a low hill. Dallas figured

the mahout was headed away to get out of sight for a few minutes where he could take care of some bathroom duties. That was not the case, however.

"Ayeee, Boss," Halim yelled. "Come see what I find."

Dallas trotted to the mahout. The day was becoming hotter and he couldn't fathom what the skinny man could possibly have discovered worthy of moving faster than necessary.

Halim was excitedly pointing a finger to the ground and generally dancing in one spot. "Here, Boss, here they are!"

When Dallas stood and looked at what had so excited Halim, he felt the nape of his neck chill. After examining the area he said, "There's at least a dozen sets of unshod tracks, and they're all recent, really fresh. I'm guessing they showed up here not long after Poxon and Latts took off. From the looks of things, the Apache are heading after them."

"We have thrilling times, Boss."

"More so than I care for, Halim." Dallas gave the horizon a quick scan, seeing nothing moving but a pair of spindly dust devils. "Let's go inform the others that we've acquired a passel of bloodthirsty renegade Apache Indians joining us in our little manhunt."

Chapter 37

Dull Knife, who had been a sub-chief among the Apache led by the fierce Geronimo, sat on his pinto alongside of his cousin, War Hawk, carefully studying the disabled stagecoach. They had found it was never wise to trust the white eyes in any matter. It might be a trap.

Geronimo had surrendered once again with a promise that the People would be fairly treated. Now the great chief was in chains and most of the Apache were being sent to some faraway land called Florida. This was a terrible thing to have happen to them, to be forced from the land where they had roamed free since the Great Spirit had walked the earth. Now there was nothing to do but kill as many of the *Pinda-Lik-O-Yi* as possible. But the task was a daunting one. These days the white eyes covered the sacred mountains and valleys thick as fleas on a buffalo robe.

"I do not believe it is a trap," Dull Knife finally said, enjoying speaking in his native tongue instead of the English they made them use on the reservation they had escaped from. "The wagon for people has broken by itself."

"Yes, my cousin." War Hawk pointed to the two horses. "The white eyes has taken the good horses and ridden them away."

"Let us go investigate this broken wagon. We must walk so as not to leave any tracks. I think maybe there might be some things of value left behind."

Moments later Dull Knife and War Hawk were poking through the stagecoach.

"They left many clothes I do not like." War Hawk was pawing through the contents of a trunk. He held up a small hand mirror and admired his war paint. "I will keep this, it is a good omen to find a looking glass."

Dull Knife found a framed photogravure of a pretty young woman; he yelled and slammed shut the lid of the trunk. "Ayeee, the white eyes have captured a spirit woman and imprisoned her behind glass."

War Hawk tucked away the mirror he had barely managed to keep hold of when his cousin had become so upset. "It is only a likeness. The Pinda-Lik-O-Yi have many of these. You are too easily frightened, my cousin."

"There is much good reason to fear them. Never do they speak the truth. Even the words on paper, signed by Geronimo, change their meaning like the weather."

"I have a good looking glass."

"We must leave the rest of these things. I do not wish to accidentally break a likeness. To release the spirit of a witch would be a bad thing, especially if she is an evil witch."

War Hawk nodded his agreement and motioned to the two horses. "We should take them. They are valuable."

"No, my cousin, we must leave them here. All of our warriors have good mounts and those horses are tired and hungry. The white eyes who left this broken people wagon have surely not gone far. I think we should ride like the wind and catch up with them, then kill them as a lesson for all white eyes to leave our land."

War Hawk shrugged. "That has been tried many times. It does not work. But to kill them is a sound idea. Rubbing out any of the Pinda-Lik-O-Yi is always a good idea."

"Let us go avenge our slain brothers, our great chief Geronimo, and all of the People that are being sent to Florida."

Moments later the two Apache had rejoined their ragtag band of renegades, told them of their quest, and quickly begun riding west on the trail of two white men with the intent of making examples out of them. Very explicit examples.

Chapter 38

"There's no doubt about it." Dallas Handley stood alongside Halim as he described the tracks the mahout had discovered. "The Apache renegades that probably attacked that way station were here, and not long ago."

Barney's brow wrinkled with concern. "How many of 'em are there, son?"

"From the tracks I saw, most likely no more than a dozen, but you know how to figure Apaches as well as anyone."

Omar gave the grizzled old man a quizzical look. "What do you mean?"

"The Apache warriors sort of come and go as they please. Especially the renegades from off a reservation. If some of them get tired, hungry, or lonely for their squaws, they just ride home." Barney took a moment to flick ash from his cigar. "On the other side of the coin, a baker's dozen of young bucks with an itch to prove their manhood might ride up an' join 'em any old time."

Dallas said, "What my dad's taking a mouthful of words to say is that twelve or so Apaches here an hour or two ago might be six or eight or fifty once we catch up with them. Behavior like that's why the Army's had such fits keeping them under control. If a person adds in the fact they can live off the land for weeks on end where a coyote would starve out, and those redskins move about being darn near invisible while making as much racket as a shadow, you get some idea as to why folks out here will feel better with them living in Florida."

Barney snorted. "And you call *me* wordy. I've known stump preachers who could save every soul in an entire town with less verbosity than you just subjected us to."

Omar Lassiter looked about worriedly. "You're *sure* they've gone?"

"Ain't noticed anyone stuck full of arrows." Barney quit chewing on his cigar to check the loads in his Colt. "That's about the surest way to tell when they're about."

"Perhaps"—Omar focused his gaze toward the eastern horizon—"the Apache might take better care of Tiberius Poxon and Harry Latts than we would. I would think having them skinned alive would fit their crimes better than hanging them."

"Dear," Mabel scolded, "that is not a Christian attitude."

Omar sighed. "You are right, of course. A nice legal hanging is also good for business. A person needs to remind themselves of what's important."

Dallas motioned to the circus wagon. "Everyone needs to keep a rifle handy now that we know the Apache are heading for Poxon and Latts. It'll likely just be a matter of time until we all get really well acquainted."

"Sure wish that thing could move faster," Barney said with a nod to the huge wagon. "Otherwise those redskins just might put a smile on Omar's face by having those two fairly well peeled by the time we get caught up with 'em."

Dallas added with a sigh, "And if they make a run for it across the desert, we're out of luck. I'd hate to have come this far only to lose out on settling with those two. I have a special peeve with Tiberius Poxon. Be a shame to head home without knowing for certain he's turned buzzard bait."

"Let's get to moving then." Omar started toward his traveling home.

"Uh, Boss," Halim said, a sandaled foot nervously kicking up dust.

"Spit it out." Omar stopped and turned to the mahout. "Those two killed a lot of good folks along with a little girl and I want them to pay for it. We'll listen to any plan that might work."

Halim gave a thin grin. "Well, Boss, like they say in Brooklyn, 'Here goes nothing.'"

"If I'd known this elephant could move so blamed fast not having to pull that big circus wagon," Dallas said grasping onto one of the ropes wrapped around the elephant, "we could have caught up with Poxon and Latts long ago."

Barney turned around and looked at his son, a beaming smile on his white-bearded face. "The way things are going, we'll be in El Paso in time for supper. I just hope he don't go and tucker out on us."

Halim brought up his legs, turned around, and faced them while squatting. "Naraka is very strong. In my country they have been known to move at a speed like this for days without stopping for rest or water. Also, he feels a bitter hate for these people we pursue. I think he blames them for poor Chitra's death."

"Reckon he's somewhat right about that. If Poxon and Latts had behaved themselves, none of this would have happened." Barney gave an uneasy look over Halim's shoulder. "Shouldn't you be watchin' the road or something?"

"Nah." The mahout shrugged dismissively. "Naraka's smart, a lot smarter than any horse. He'll keep going just like this until I give him a signal to stop. No worries, Boss. He won't do anything to cause us problems."

"If it wasn't for those steam trains coming to be all over . . . " Barney said. He hesitated long enough to assure himself a movement he noticed in a clump of greasewood bushes was only a jackrabbit before continuing. "I'd venture elephants could catch on here in Texas. Be a lot more interesting to have around than horses."

"They become tiresome, Boss," Halim said. "You can trust me on this."

Dallas nodded. "I'm sorry Omar couldn't have come along, but I reckon there's only so much room even on an elephant."

"He needed to stay with his wife anyway," Barney said. "A pretty little lady like her needs protecting, especially in wild country."

Halim chuckled. "Boss, one of Princess Noria's acts in the circus is a trick shooter with a rifle. She can part your hair with a bullet from a block away and not singe your scalp."

Dallas said, "Reckon we should have left my dad behind and brought her along. Pa's eyesight's getting so bad, he'll most likely use up all of his ammo and not hit anything vital. Besides, Mabel's a lot better on the eyes."

Barney checked the loads in his Winchester rifle for the third time. "Sonny boy, you'd best recall just how handy Omar is with a knife before making any eyes at the cute wife of his."

"No worries, Boss." Halim spun around to face ahead. He said over his shoulder, "Omar's not the jealous type. As long as I've been with his circus, I can only remember a couple of men he's stabbed that took it serious enough to croak. Most of 'em just wind up with a big doctor bill."

"I'd reckon having a pretty wife would carry a curse along with it, considering on the matter." Barney fished one of the long black cigars Omar had given them for their trek from his shirt pocket, then frowned when he realized he'd forgotten to bring along any matches. "But all things being equal, I could live with a curse like that."

"I have a wife in India," Halim volunteered, bringing incredulous looks to both Barney and Dallas. "I would like someday to see if she is pretty."

"Don't you know?" Dallas asked. "Most men take note of things like that."

"Never met her, Boss. My pap and her pap set it all up a long time ago." He shrugged. "That's how it's done over there. My pap got two elephants, a nice wagon, and some sheep for taking her off their hands. Girls in India are to be gotten rid of as quick as possible."

Barney lowered an eyebrow. "Just how old were you when you got saddled with a wife, for Pete's sake?"

Halim cocked his head in thought. "I was eight years of age, Boss. Pap boarded her out in school until I got back from college." He chuckled. "I think my pap has paid out more than he bargained for. I've been over here for a long time."

"Hard to believe you've never set eyes on her." Barney shook his head. "She might be cuter than a speckled pup."

"Or she could be a shrew." Halim studied the horizon. The sun was low, it would not be long until it would set. "Or both pretty and a shrew. That is how they come sometimes."

"Reckon females in India ain't a lot different from the variety we have to deal with here," Barney said. "Except that it's a lot easier for 'em to get hitched over there, and at a nice early age too. In this county gettin' married is a task women really work hard at."

"Noticed that, Boss," Halim said. "Had a gal in Brooklyn chase after me for two years before I married her."

Dallas choked. "You're married *twice.*"

"Nah, Boss. I been married four times, not counting the one my pap has waiting for me in India. American women like to get married. All I had to do was ask 'em."

Barney said, "They generally expect you to stick around."

Halim gave a sigh. "Ain't it the truth, Boss. Dodging them isn't easy, but I get the job done. Following after a circus isn't an easy task."

Dallas and Barney Handley looked at each other and decided to drop the matter. Foreigners, especially circus performers, certainly had a strange way of looking at things. The two men grew silent and studied the landscape for danger as they made a rapid pace across the bleak desert in pursuit of two men they hoped to kill before the Apache beat them to it.

Chapter 39

Dull Knife was crouching low behind a large clump of creosote bushes, sorting through the collection of arrows in his quiver. He grunted with displeasure at the quality of arrowheads he was forced to deal with these days. Dull Knife grudgingly accepted the fact that the white eyes' rifles were much more efficient, but the sound of thunder they made could be heard for a long distance in the treeless desert. Sometimes that attracted the wrong kind of attention. Since they were close to a road, the quieter they remained, the better.

War Hawk, who was beside him, said, "The Pinda-Lik-O-Yi we pursue are idiots. They stay on the road and their horses are tired, yet they push them almost to the death. I think any man who does this to horses should be shot."

"That *is* our plan," Dull Knife said, selecting what he thought to be the sharpest arrow of the lot. "I wish the braves had joined us in this battle. Now we are but two."

"They wanted to go south of the border and kill Mexicans." War Hawk hefted his bow to make certain all was in readiness. His cousin being so picky with arrows was a peeve. The arrows always did what they were meant to do. "I also would like to go to Mexico. After we have made an example of these two white eyes, I think maybe we should do that."

"Perhaps you are right, my cousin. Soon we will also have more horses to sell. I will have three, you will have one."

War Hawk's eyes narrowed. "I am your cousin."

"That is true. But I am a sub-chief under Geromino. Any warrior of the Apache always honors his chief."

"Geronimo's on his way to Florida. I hear it never snows there, but I believe that is another lie of the white eyes. I claim two horses as my due. There are two of us and four horses to steal. I do not think you are fair to claim three horses."

Dull Knife snarled, "My cousin refuses to honor the ways of our fathers. I am a chief among warriors. Three horses is my just reward."

"Two horses." War Hawk held up a pair of fingers. "I claim two horses or you can wait for the Pinda-Lik-O-Yi by yourself. I will go and join our brothers, kill Mexicans, and take as many of their horses as I wish."

"You hurt me, my cousin. I only wish to keep the old ways alive. To honor our ancestors I must claim three horses. Surely you can see my point."

"I do see your point, my cousin. Now *you* can see *me* ride away. Since we were but children, you have been greedy. If you kill the white eyes by yourself, then you will have four horses. I go."

Dull Knife watched with a mix of disbelief and fury as his ungrateful cousin actually ran to his horse and rode off, leaving him alone to fight the white eyes. This explained why the Apache were being shipped to Florida. There was no honor among the warriors these days. Geronimo had failed them. The gods had failed them. Now his own cousin, War Hawk, had failed to keep the old ways. This was not a good omen.

However, the two Apache had not ridden far ahead of the white eyes to set up the ambush. He had his bow and arrows. Four horses was worth a brief wait. Then he would join his band of warriors in Mexico, where, if it took years, he would find some way to shame his cousin for deserting him on the eve of a glorious battle and refusing to show him just honor.

The dust from War Hawk's departure had not long settled before Dull Knife heard the sounds of approaching horses. He had planned this attack well. Here the road dropped down from a mesa, made a bend, then ascended up another hill. The white eyes could not see the Apache until they were only a short distance away. The fact was not lost on Dull Knife that he also could not see his enemy until they were quite close.

The sub-chief felt his heart quicken. He fought the urge to run out and meet the enemy face-to-face in glorious battle. But there were none of the People here to witness his bravery. It would be wiser to wait until the white eyes were very close, then shoot them full of arrows. It would also be a lot safer.

From his hiding place among the stunted creosote bushes Dull Knife watched as the two hated Pinda-Lik-O-Yi dropped from the flat mesa and came into view. They were moving much too slow. Something was wrong. Then, he noticed that the horse one of the men was riding had thrown a shoe. This was not an uncommon occurrence. The Apache had better sense than to nail pieces of steel to their horses' hooves.

But the incident had stopped the white eyes out of range of his bow and arrow. This was another bad omen.

Dull Knife began slithering closer. The stupid white eyes were paying full attention to their dilemma, ignoring the danger. War Hawk had been correct about one thing: They *were* idiots.

"Well, well, Mr. Latts." Tiberius Poxon clucked his tongue and frowned at the lame gelding. "It appears that your luck with horses has not improved. I suggest we leave it and you ride the other one."

"Yes, sir, I really would like to shoot the thing for causing you problems, but I don't think firing a gun would be a good idea. There are Apache about, you know."

"They are a cowardly race, Mr. Latts. The closer we get to El Paso, the less likelihood we have of encountering them."

"We have been making good time. I'd reckon that we're only fifty miles from there, or maybe even less. Should be in El Paso tonight sometime, if these horses hold out."

Tiberius Poxon glanced nervously over his shoulder. "Make haste, Mr. Latts. For some reason I feel ill at ease."

"Yes, sir." Harry Latts swung around to pull his Colt and dispatch his boss. All of that money in those brown saddlebags would set him up for life. And the loony Tiberius Poxon was absolutely correct that the closer they were to El Paso, the more difficult it would be to blame the Apache for his demise. Latts was greased lightning with a gun. The task would be completed within a heartbeat.

Dull Knife noticed that one of the Pinda-Lik-O-Yi had been wounded. A white bandage went completely around the man's head and was tied with a knot on the top of his head. There was, however, a wonderful red spot over one of the man's ears. This reminded him of the targets the soldiers were always shooting at on the reservation. They called them "bull's-eyes" for some reason that escaped him. The Apache decided it was worth going for. He wondered deeply if the imperfect arrowhead he was forced to employ was sharp enough to go all the way through the man's head. There was only one way to find out.

The warrior drew back the bow and let an arrow fly. Before he could check out the results of his shot, his attention was drawn to a huge gray shape that had suddenly appeared on the edge of the hill above him.

No Apache ever screamed from sheer terror. Certainly no warrior did.

Dull Knife screamed. He bolted erect, his every nerve on fire with pure raw horror. The Apache panicked, dropped the bow and arrow, then dashed sobbing for his horse so that he could run away from the dreadful giant monster that had appeared to kill him and steal his soul. It was surely a demon from Hell. The white-eyes preachers had been right about such things. There really is a Devil.

Chapter 40

Tiberius Poxon's dark eyes widened and sparked in the light of a dying sun when he spun at the unmistakable smacking of an arrow piercing flesh and bone. It was a distinct popping sound, like when a person bites down hard on a piece of gristle.

Harry Latts sat erect in the saddle of his lame horse. The first thing Poxon took note of was the arrow that went in one of his gunman's ears and extended out the other. The second thing was the man's hand grasping the handle of his Colt. It was quite obvious Harry Latts was dead; he simply hadn't realized that fact and fallen over yet.

The man was pulling his gun to protect me, Tiberius Poxon thought. *I really misjudged his character.*

Then the mining magnate stiffened with fear at the blood-curdling scream of an Apache warrior who bolted into the open from a small copse of green bushes. To Poxon's utter amazement, the Indian dropped his bow on the ground and ran off down the draw. He could have almost sworn the Apache was sobbing with fright as he disappeared into the shadows of the mesa.

Strange. I must have scared him something awful. It is jus too bad that Apache didn't get a good look at me before he shot that arrow through poor Harry's head.

Tiberius snorted when he realized the folly of his thinking. That redskin actually did him a favor. An arrow through Latts's head could only have come from an Indian attack. He quickly scanned up and down the canyon. Thankfully, there was no sign of any more Apache. And best of all, he had been totally unscathed from the incident.

It was mere seconds after Harry Latts's body thudded onto the dry desert earth that a movement from behind caused Tiberius Poxon to turn his focus to the rim of the mesa.

"Oh, shit!" he swore, trying desperately to decide what to do.

"That certainly was unusual behavior to witness from an Apache warrior," Dallas Handley remarked. "I can't say I've ever even heard of any acting like the one we just saw running away."

Barney cocked the hammer on his Winchester. "From the looks of it, that Indian was alone. Like I've said, they're an unpredictable species, but I didn't expect them to be so blamed frightened by an elephant."

Halim turned to the man behind him. "Boss, I don't mean to be telling you how to do your job, but shouldn't someone be shooting at that fellow down there?"

"Go ahead, Dad," Dallas said. "I can't tell for sure from this distance, but he looks enough like Tiberius Poxon to use some ammo on."

"I'll send him our greetings." Barney leveled the Winchester at the figure on horseback and pulled the trigger.

* * *

The cloud of smoke from the shot was still hanging in the air when Barney extricated himself from a greasewood bush in time to watch a panicked elephant head back over the rimrock.

Dallas stood up and dusted himself off. "I reckon Halim was right about elephants not taking over from horses. They're too excitable."

"I don't think Naraka has ever had a gun fired from behind his head before." Halim winced as he pulled a piece of cholla cactus from his leg. "The noise frightened him very much."

"I noticed that." Barney stood slowly shaking himself to make certain nothing was broken, then began inspecting his Winchester. "Elephants do have mighty big ears. Reckon there was a clue we failed to take note of."

"Did you hit him, Dad?" Dallas asked, peering into the shadowy canyon.

"Of course I did, sonny boy. Your ole pa always hits what he aims at."

"I must go after Naraka." Halim plucked the last of the cactus stickers from his leg. "He will not run far away." The mahout added after a moment, "At least I don't think so. But this is a new experience for him."

"A person could say the same thing about this whole blasted manhunt." Dallas gingerly fished his rifle from where it had fallen into a patch of prickly pear cactus. "If I thought there would be more bounty hunts like this one, I'd become a corset salesman in San Angelo."

Barney snorted. "You ought to give that some thought, sonny boy. The pain from having all those females slapping you would be worse than getting tossed off a spooked elephant." He studied the shadowy draw with a cautious eye. "While Halim chases after our transportation, let's go check out who all got shot."

The mahout said, "I will return as quickly as I can, Boss." He turned and painfully hobbled away.

"I'd advise caution, Dad," Dallas said after blowing dirt from the hammer of his rifle. "Outlaws can be tricky to deal with."

Barney shrugged. "Why take a chance? Ammo's cheaper than doctors. Let's just shoot another hole in 'em."

"We'll just do that," Dallas agreed. Then the duo began to carefully make their way down into the shadowy draw.

Dull Knife, in his terror to escape the huge Devil the Pinda-Lik-O-Yi had unleashed to kill him and snatch away his soul to burn forever in the white man's hell, had chosen to force his horse up a steep rocky draw to the main road. He wanted to come out well behind where the beast had stood on the rimrock.

The frightened Apache now wanted more than anything to reach the sanctuary of the reservation. Joining Geronimo in Florida now seemed like a grand idea.

No sooner had Dull Knife ridden onto the road than his worst nightmares became realized. With a trumpeting scream only a demon could muster, the huge beast that was big as a wagon and had teeth longer than a man, came charging at him from a cloud of dust.

A few seconds of frozen hesitation gave Dull Knife no exit. The gray beast hit his mount a solid blow, knocking both horse and rider over the edge of the cliff. The last thought the Apache had before being crushed to death beneath his horse was to wonder if it really never did snow in the land called Florida.

* * *

"Now what kind of fresh hell has struck?" Dallas said as he and his father spun at the sound of a trumpeting elephant to watch both an Indian and his horse come crashing down the side of the canyon about a quarter mile from where they stood.

"Looks like our Apache went and found that elephant we lost," Barney said. "I'd venture most folks could live in Texas for a lifetime and never witness another event like that one."

Dallas shrugged. "At least we don't have anything more to fret from that Indian."

Barney stared ahead. The lowering sun was casting dark shadows about the rocky chasm. "Let's move with caution here, sonny boy. I've got a distinctly bad feeling about this."

Dallas felt a chill creeping down his spine. "Yeah, Dad. I feel the same way."

"Let's agree to shoot the first thing that moves."

"Yeah. Several times."

Carefully the pair made their way into the murky depths of the strangely silent canyon.

Chapter 41

"Reckon you're right about not wasting a perfectly good bullet, Dad. This man's dead as any doornail I've ever come across." Dallas Handley clucked his tongue and studied the corpse. "My guess is this fellow's Harry Latts. I've heard him described as being skinny with a pockmarked face."

Barney said, "Sure is something how that arrow went plumb through his head like it did. Mostly, Indians shoot for the chest. An ear makes for a mighty small target."

"You've made a point of telling us how unpredictable the Apache are."

"They are that, sonny boy."

"Well, he hit what he was aiming for most likely." Dallas nodded to a dead horse lying draped across a large rock. "That's more than I can say for your shooting abilities."

"Ain't my fault. The elephant was jittering around too much for me to draw a true bead."

Dallas sighed. "Now of the two horses we have left alive, one's lame and the other is plumb tuckered out and almost dying of thirst. From the looks of things,

Tiberius Poxon simply rode away nice and peaceful-like while we were picking ourselves up off the ground."

"Don't blame me, sonny boy. If I'd had any notion that elephant would go nutty as a peach-orchard boar over a little ol' gunshot, I'd have climbed down and went some distance away to start shooting." Barney fished a long nine cigar from his vest. He frowned when he discovered it had been broken from the fall. Then he remembered he didn't have any matches to light one with anyway, so he bit off a healthy portion to chew. "If I hadn't had to contend with a nervous elephant, I'd have plugged the man I was aiming for instead of shooting his packhorse by pure accident."

"When we get back to San Angelo, you're going to see an eye doc and get fitted for spectacles."

Barney Handley ignored his son. A thought had struck. "I'm going to check out the saddlebags on that dead horse. We might get lucky enough to find some decent cigars, or maybe a tin of matches."

A moment later Barney rose from the dead horse and turned to Dallas; his eyes were wide as he held out a double handful of twenty-dollar gold pieces to glisten in the last light of day. "Sonny boy, there's enough money in these bags to buy not just those cigars and matches, but the store selling them."

Dallas bent down and cut away the saddlebags from the horse. He took a few minutes to study the contents. "There's not only a small fortune in gold and paper money here, Dad, but it looks like there are signed deeds to every mine and business building in Devil's Gate." He shook his head in disbelief. "I can't figure Poxon not recording them in his name. The assignments are all notarized from the sellers' signatures, but the buyers' lines are blank."

"You're a-telling me anyone can write in their name and own what's on the deed."

"Yeah, that's *exactly* what I'm saying. Every thing Tiberius Poxon killed for, bullied people out of, or plain stole is probably here."

Barney smiled at the gold coins in his hands. "I can make out the name of Handley on these plain as day."

"We need to turn the deeds over to the law. There will be a lot of good folks mighty glad to get their property back." Dallas chewed on his lower lip. "But cash money always causes problems. Everyone gets greedy and claims it for themselves when they hold no rightful ownership. That Sheriff Wilson took away and tossed a two-thousand-dollar outlaw's head I had into his stove. I'm thinking maybe keeping what's due me is only right. And you've been out a lot of time and expense."

"Sound thinking, sonny boy. I'm glad all of my good upbringing took."

Dallas scanned the canyon with a worried brow. "Dad, I've dealt with outlaws and crooks for a lot of years. Tiberius Poxon's entire fortune is here. I'm of the mind he ain't going to simply run off and leave it; that's not a normal response. He got spooked and moved off to save his hide, but you can bet he didn't go very far. That fellow's planning to come back and kill us."

Barney snorted. "I thought *we* were chasing after *him*."

"It's one of the oldest tricks in the book, circle around and come in from a person's backside. I've likely plugged over a dozen outlaws using that tactic."

Barney filled his pockets with gold coins, then retrieved his Winchester from where he had left it leaning in the crotch of a scraggly mesquite tree. "Tiberius Poxon can't come from our backside because of the canyon wall. But I do reckon he could have gone either up or down the draw. Hard to say. Maybe he's just feeling so lucky to be alive that he's planning on riding like the wind to El Paso and start over where no one knows him."

Dallas clucked his tongue. "Greed is what causes most folks to become crooks. No, Dad, Tiberius Poxon's not far off. That man is going to come for his money and deeds."

"What I can't figure is why those deeds were left open where anyone holding the paper can own the property. I never heard of the like. Most people file those things with the courthouse before the ink's dry."

"Let's watch our backsides and don't look a gift horse in the mouth. Poxon has killed a lot of good people for the contents of those saddlebags."

Barney's eyes narrowed to slits as he scanned first up, then down the rugged canyon. "That feller's never dealt with the Handleys before. Poxon's a dead man if he comes after us."

Dallas gave a thin smile while sizing up which large rocks to use as protection from an attack. "I think you're right on both counts, Dad. Let's just hope we can get that fellow killed in short order. This manhunt has gone on long enough to become tiresome."

In the bloody glow of a dying day, Tiberius Poxon stood alongside his horse, glaring with hate-filled eyes at the battered and broken bodies of an Apache warrior and his horse.

Poxon had seen the circus elephant panic when one of the men who were riding it shot at him and killed his packhorse. He had quickly ducked and ridden down the canyon to find shelter. Thinking back on the matter, he should have attacked his pursuers the second they had been thrown from the elephant. Instead, he chose to run. Then, this Apache and his horse came crashing down the cliff and nearly hit him.

At least there are no more Apache about, Tiberius thought. *That elephant scared this one worse than a company of cavalry.*

Calming now, he remembered he had seen only two armed men on the elephant. The little man wearing a turban was just along to drive the beast. This gave him hope. He knew all of the men were on foot, possibly even injured. That would be wonderful. Certainly they would not expect him to sneak up and kill them. And this was what he had to do. If he didn't recover those deeds, his life wouldn't be worth a plugged nickel. The man who had financed the taking over of Devil's Gate and its rich silver mines wasn't the type of person to be understanding of failure. Not understanding at all. Politicians never were.

It was simply too bad Harry Latts had let him down. If the gunman had been competent, he would have been able to help recover those precious saddlebags instead of simply dying worthlessly.

No matter. Tiberius Poxon was good enough with a gun to handle the situation. He turned to climb back on his horse, then froze with fear. The mining magnate knew he was looking at his own death.

Chapter 42

The fires of a bloody sunset reflected like red ice in War Hawk's flint eyes as he, along with six more Apache warriors, stood with weapons at the ready, silently regarding Tiberius Poxon.

"I came to see if I could help your friend," Tiberius said with a voice that he realized came across more like a plea than a statement. "But, as you can see, he is unfortunately dead."

After a long moment of silence War Hawk spoke. His English was quite good from years of living on a reservation. "You have killed my cousin, Dull Knife."

"No!" Poxon nearly screamed. "He fell off that cliff."

"All white eyes are liars. No Apache ever would fall off a cliff by accident. We heard a gunshot. You shot our sub-chief from ambush. Then you came here to steal anything of value."

A warrior snorted. "We were coming to help our fallen Dull Knife steal some horses. To shoot a man from hiding is a very cowardly thing to do."

"But I didn't shoot him!" Tiberius Poxon felt fear rising inside him like bile. "Look at the body, for God's sake. There's no bullet holes in it."

War Hawk eyed his cousin's battered corpse. "He is

pretty badly messed up." Then he walked to Dull Knife and gave the bloody, crushed body a brief scrutiny. "I think there could be a dozen bullet holes in him and we could not know."

A warrior to Poxon's left shook a bowie knife. "This man lies. All white eyes lie. It will snow in the land of Florida. Geronimo will tell us this when he returns, as he surely will."

"Take his guns and then bind his hands with thongs," War Hawk ordered. "This man claims he did not shoot from hiding like a coward. I say we let him prove his bravery."

Tiberius Poxon held his hands straight out to his sides and allowed a pair of warriors to take his weapons. He felt strangely relieved that the Indians were going to test him. Whatever proof they required that he was no coward, he would gladly consent to. He just wanted to have this childish test over with quickly as possible and get on with the business of recovering the lost saddlebags containing his future.

"I will accept your challenge," Poxon said with more determination than he felt.

War Hawk gave him a cold stare. "We are not giving you a choice here, white eyes. I do not think you are brave at all. The test will not last the night, I fear."

"All night!" Tiberius shouted. "I can't take that long. There's . . . business I must attend to."

"Ah, yes," War Hawk said, "all Pinda-Lik-O-Yi, as the People call your race, are always concerned about 'business.' And now, the Apache will be about *their* business." He turned to a warrior. "Yellow Dog, go bring me my case from my pony."

The skinny Indian turned and dashed off down the canyon.

"Naiche, Spotted Elk," War Hawk said, nodding his head at a pair of mesquite trees. "Remove this brave man's shirt and tie him to those trees, one arm to each." He grinned evilly. "And make the bindings tight. Our brave white man wishes to prove he is a warrior. I would not wish to disappoint him with soft treatment."

A few moments later Tiberius Poxon had been stripped naked to his waist and securely bound tight between the trees with painful leather thongs. "Let's get on with this. I'm a busy man."

War Hawk nodded. "Tie his legs also. I think that will be necessary."

Poxon had no choice but to submit.

The warrior Yellow Dog came and handed War Hawk a round leather packet. When the Apache unrolled it on the top of a red sandstone rock, Tiberius Poxon's eyes widened with primal fear. In the last light of day, a pair of surgical scalpels glistened against brown leather.

"Wha . . . what are you going to do?" Poxon's throat was so dry he could barely speak.

War hawk selected the scalpel with an ivory handle that he favored and held it up. "The Apache admire bravery above all else. I will start with your back. At first only a small strip of your skin will be removed. If you are truly brave and do not cry out, then I take more skin, maybe from your arms, or face. The test is not to kill, white eyes, only to prove that you can stand pain like a warrior. If you do not cry out, we will believe you did not shoot Dull Knife and release you. But if you wail like a hurt dog, we then will know you lie and kill you. Very slowly."

For the first time in his life Tiberius Poxon felt the same sheer bone-chilling terror coursing through his being that he had caused in so many others.

"You were right about catching a flash of light off something metal," Dallas said, returning to his father's side. "It came off a knife held by an Indian."

"How many of 'em are there this time?" Barney shook his head in disgust. "I'll tell you, sonny boy, there's been enough problems plaguing us without more pesky Apache showing up."

"I counted seven. What's more interesting is the fact they've got Tiberius Poxon. My guess is they're thinking he killed the Indian that got knocked off the cliff by the elephant."

Barney grinned knowingly. "Well, there was a gunshot, then they find their buddy all crumpled and dead. I'm of the opinion those Apache *are* feeling rather wrathy."

"I saw them rip off Poxon's shirt and tie him between a couple of trees. Then I figured I'd get back here before it starts getting dark. There's still going to be a full moon tonight so it won't slow the Apaches down any, but I didn't want to risk stumbling over a rock or a stick and let them know we're about."

"If Halim comes back riding that elephant, it'll be difficult not to notice."

Dallas cocked his head. "I reckon if all Apache are as scared of elephants as the one that ran off screaming his tonsils out, we shouldn't have us a problem."

Barney gave a sad sigh and watched as the final red rays of sunlight surrendered to the beginning night. "Life takes some odd twists and turns, son. Remember when Omar Lassiter said that if Tiberius Poxon were to be skinned alive by Indians, it would be fitting justice for all of the terrible things he'd done to people? Then Omar thought on the matter and decided the passage in the Good Book about letting God settle matters was the way to go and let his hate rest."

Dallas bummed a broken piece of cigar from his father, then bit off a chew. "Just as well we don't have any matches. The Apache can smell smoke for miles. But I'd say Poxon's going to suffer worse than most before he cashes in his chips. And there's honestly nothing we could do about it even if we were so inclined. Seven Apache warriors are a handful."

"I'm hoping Halim doesn't run into problems. That little guy's a likable sort. He should have figured out earlier that elephants get rather spooked over gunshots, however."

"My guess is he'll be fine. Those Apache have their attentions on Poxon. I'm also of the opinion that he won't take being peeled very well. If he starts howling with pain right off, they'll figure he's not brave enough to be worthy of keeping alive very long."

Barney Handley began to say something when the shrill scream of a man in agony echoed off the steep canyon walls.

"Well, that sure didn't take long," Barney said. He couldn't help but wince. Any man long on the frontier knew to dread being captured by Indians worse than rattlesnakes or gunshot wounds. "Tiberius Poxon's turning out to be a disappointment to those warriors."

Dallas gave a low sigh. "The Apache don't have any use for cowards." He spit a wad of tobacco at a passing vinegarroon. "It's an odd fact of life that those who cause the most pain can't take it when they're on the receiving end."

Another scream of agony echoed off sandstone cliffs. Dallas and Barney Handley sat side by side leaning against a large flat rock. They chewed their tobacco and listened to the shrieks and cries of a man being skinned alive. After a while, the screams sounded like nothing human.

Chapter 43

The baking dry heat of another West Texas summer day was just beginning to build when Halim came riding Naraka down the rocky ravine. He had seen Dallas and Barney from the road above where it passed along the edge of the high rimrocks.

Halim cocked his head at the two rounded mounds of dirt that were most certainly graves. He took note of the second dead horse he had encountered since descending into the depth of the canyon, then slid down the rope wrapped around the elephant's neck and scurried over to join his friends.

"Sorry to be gone so long, Boss," the mahout said. "Naraka was more frightened than I'd thought. He ran many miles away, but now he seems calm as ever."

Barney straightened and shifted from side to side to work a kink out of his back. "Let's take care to keep him that way. It's a fair walk to anywhere from here."

Dallas Handley nodded at the graves. "Tiberius Poxon's under one pile, an Indian's under the other. Since we had some time on our hands we went ahead and buried the both of them."

"Did you kill Mr. Poxon?" Hailm asked.

"Nope." Barney shook his head. "The Apache did. Took 'em most of the night to do it too. They thought he'd shot the warrior we just covered over. Actually that elephant of yours did the deed, but we're pleased with the results."

"These Apache." Halim's voice showed concern. "They are gone now?"

"Yeah," Dallas said. "And it appears they're considerably spooked by elephants so I don't reckon they'll trouble us any now that you're back."

Halim noticed an odd-looking fuzzy black and red bug that appeared to be sunning itself on the top of a white rock. He picked it up, frowned, then handed it over to Dallas.

"That's one of Tiberius Poxon's eyelids," the bounty hunter said matter-of-factly. "Too bad we missed it." Then he tossed the gruesome item onto the nearest grave.

"I think I will return to India," the mahout said. "At the very least, I know I will leave Texas."

"Lots better country here, now that Poxon's pushing up cactus," Barney said with a shrug. "At least it will be better until someone just as bad comes along and takes his place."

"Things are not much different in India, Boss, bad people everywhere." Halim motioned to the waiting elephant. "We should go. The nearest water is Mr. Lassiter's traveling home."

Dallas shrugged and draped an obviously heavy pair of brown leather saddlebags over his shoulders. "There's no reason to stick around here."

After the three men were sitting atop the elephant, Halim touched his wand to Naraka's forehead and started the huge elephant trudging his way from the craggy canyon. After a moment he turned to Dallas and Barney. "You are now returning home to San Angelo?"

"Dad will be," Dallas said. There was a sadness to his voice the mahout had never noticed before. "I'm going back to Devil's Gate. I made a lady there a promise. I intend to keep it."

Halim smiled. "Ah, an affair of the heart."

"You might say that," the bounty hunter said; his mouth felt dry as the dusty ground upon which they traveled. "The girl's name is Velvet Dawn. She saved my life, then Tiberius Poxon ordered her hung in my place. I promised her I'd return and take her away from Devil's Gate. I'd give anything if it wasn't inside a coffin, but a promise is something to honor."

The mahout nodded, then spun to face ahead. He felt a burning lump building in his throat. There really was nothing more to say. With a gentle tap from his wand, Naraka speeded his pace across the barren countryside.

As the three men passed along the high rimrock above the fresh graves, not one gave so much as a passing glance at the final resting place of the mining magnate, Tiberius Poxon. It would be a long time before the man's evil deeds were forgotten. But the time for healing had begun.

Epilogue

When Dallas Handley returned to Devil's Gate, he was only mildly surprised to find Frank Dutton the new sheriff. The former railroad detective explained he was getting tired of all of the traveling.

Dallas suspected having a few cannons to enjoy was the main reason for him changing jobs. Dutton only had to shoot a couple of toughs, and rough up a dozen or so more, before Devil's Gate became as peaceful a town as could be found in Texas. With the reward money from Jasper Flatt's bounty, which Dallas was nice enough to let him keep, he built a comfortable house where Tiberius Poxon's mansion had once stood and sent for his family.

The deeds Dallas had brought back made returning everyone's rightful property an easy task. The bounty hunter's obvious generosity and caring led to a citizens' committee being formed to pay him a substantial reward. Much to the delight of the residents, Dallas Handley only allowed a handsome brass plaque honoring his efforts to be placed on the front of the town hall. He told the new mayor, Harry Dinkman, to use the money they had raised to build a nice brick schoolhouse for the benefit of all the children.

Omar Lassiter was quite amazed to receive a thousand dollars from the Handleys as payment for his services. The bounty hunter explained that there would most likely be a reward for Harry Latts, which was the reason they had brought along the man's head, with the arrow still sticking through it.

Mabel Washburn was quite upset over having a head to go along with a dead body inside the traveling home. Her feelings were well soothed when Dallas Handley gave them an additional thousand dollars to pay for the girl's burial and future doctor bills for Mabel's frayed nerves.

Lassiter's traveling circus moved on to Chicago, where it played successfully for months. The troupe was loaded on a train heading for Philadelphia that derailed on the outskirts of Cleveland. While the wreck killed no people, the damages threw Omar Lassiter into bankruptcy. He and Mabel were last known to be running a restaurant in New Orleans.

A new mining company bought up all of the silver mines in Devil's Gate. The engineer in charge was miffed when he had to pay Dallas Handley ten thousand dollars for his half interest in the key claim, the Forlorn Hope. What was even more expensive was the bounty hunter's condition that the mill be moved a couple of miles away, so as not to fill the town with smoke. There was no choice, however. From this time forward, the residents of Devil's Gate have enjoyed clean air.

War Hawk eventually rejoined Geronimo when the great chief was moved to Fort Sill, Oklahoma. The two warriors became close friends and drinking companions. Both toured with Pawnee Bill's Wild West Show and became quite wealthy. To this day a photograph of Geronimo driving his beloved Cadillac automobile is available from the National Archives and Records Service. The smiling Indian sitting in the front seat beside the venerable chief is War Hawk. Both were drunk at the time.

Barney Handley, upon his return to San Angelo, surprised everyone by getting a barbershop shave and haircut and buying a natty suit of clothes. He then acquired ownership of Miss Hattie's Rooming House for Wayward Girls. Even his oldest friends could not recall ever seeing him so happy.

Harry Latts's head turned out to be worthless. The judge ruled that there was no way to prove the gunman responsible for any crime. Barney placed the head in a wire cage and set it on an ant bed for a few weeks, which cleaned it up nicely. The grinning white skull with an arrow through the ears sat in a glass case on a shelf behind the ornate bar of the Concho Pearl Saloon for many years, and was quite a conversation piece.

On a section of high ground, beneath a spreading live oak tree, stands the largest white-marble tombstone in the San Angelo Cemetery. Atop the monument is a beautiful angel with spread wings. The inscription reads simply in large letters etched deep into the stone: VELVET 1886

Everyone who comes across the monument wonders about the odd inscription, but for some strange reason neither the man who paid for the expensive stone will talk about it, nor will his father. Barney Handley will only say that a good woman lies there, then change the subject. Dallas Handley gets a faraway look in his eye, then walks away.

But no one denies the stone is an impressive one, and all are proud to have it gracing the San Angelo, Texas, Cemetery.